For Diana,

Even in darkness, there is light...

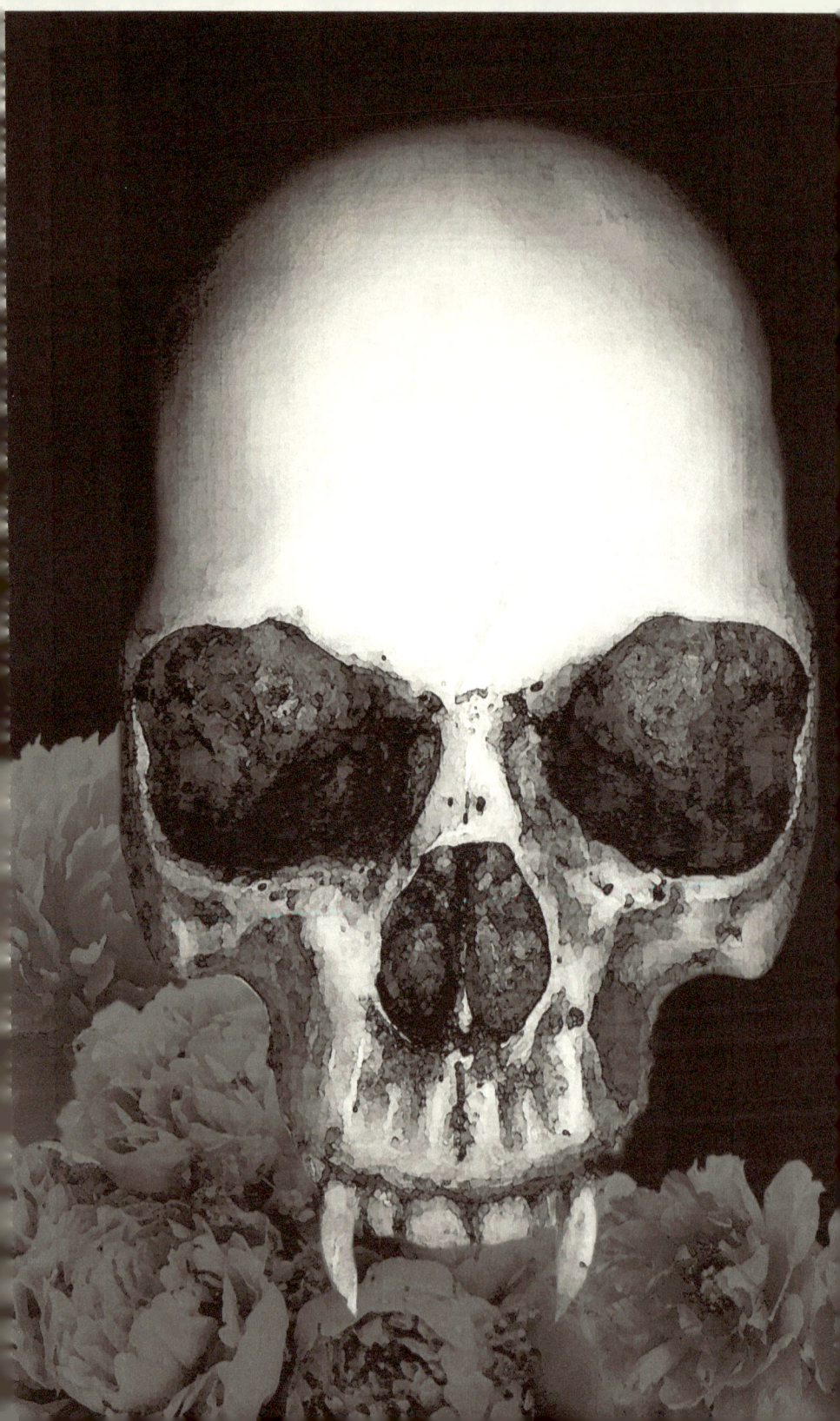

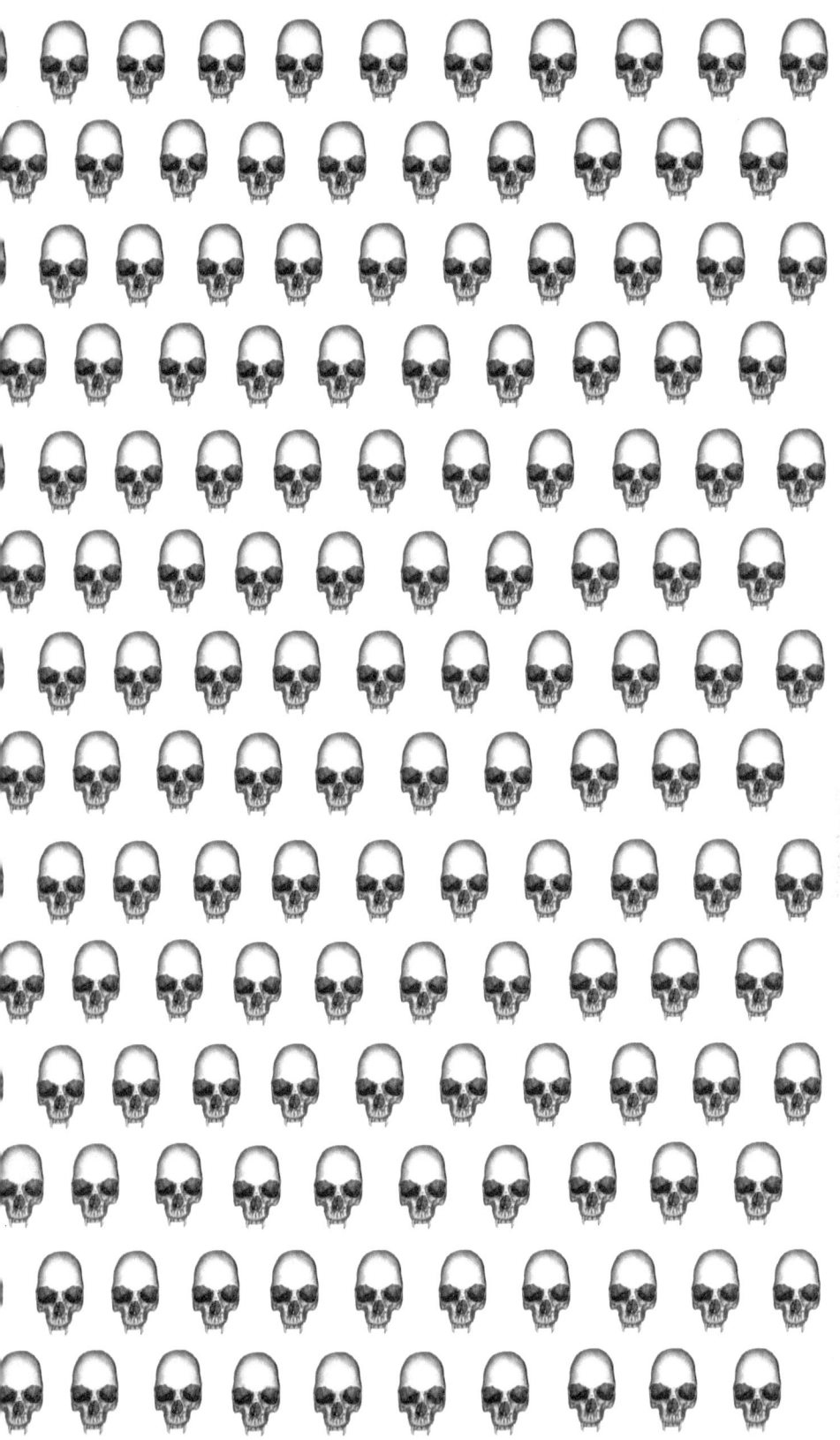

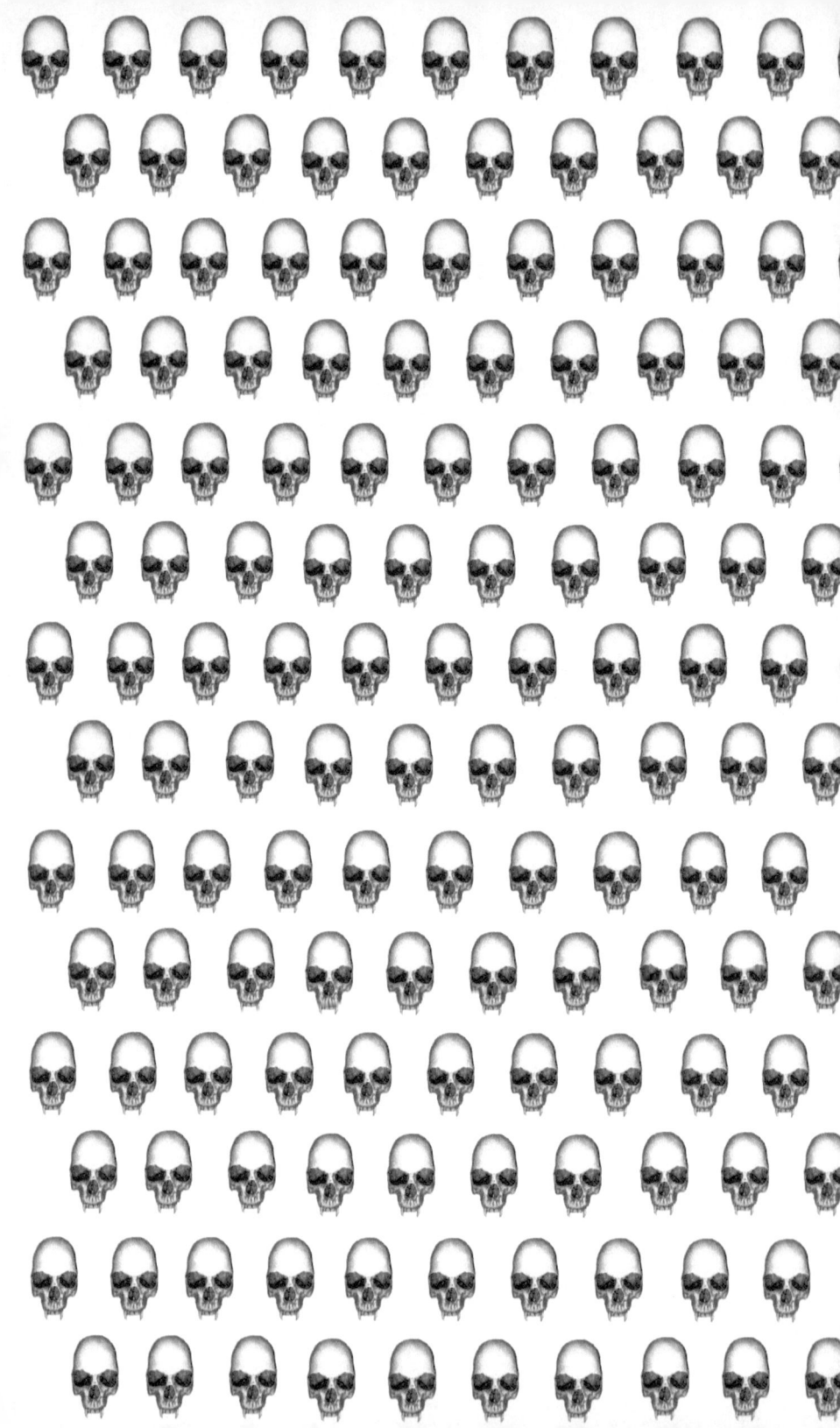

WOLFGANG

F. D. GROSS

Written by F. D. Gross
Edited by Deborah DeNicola

Published by arrangement with the author
ISBN: 978-1-62217-995-4

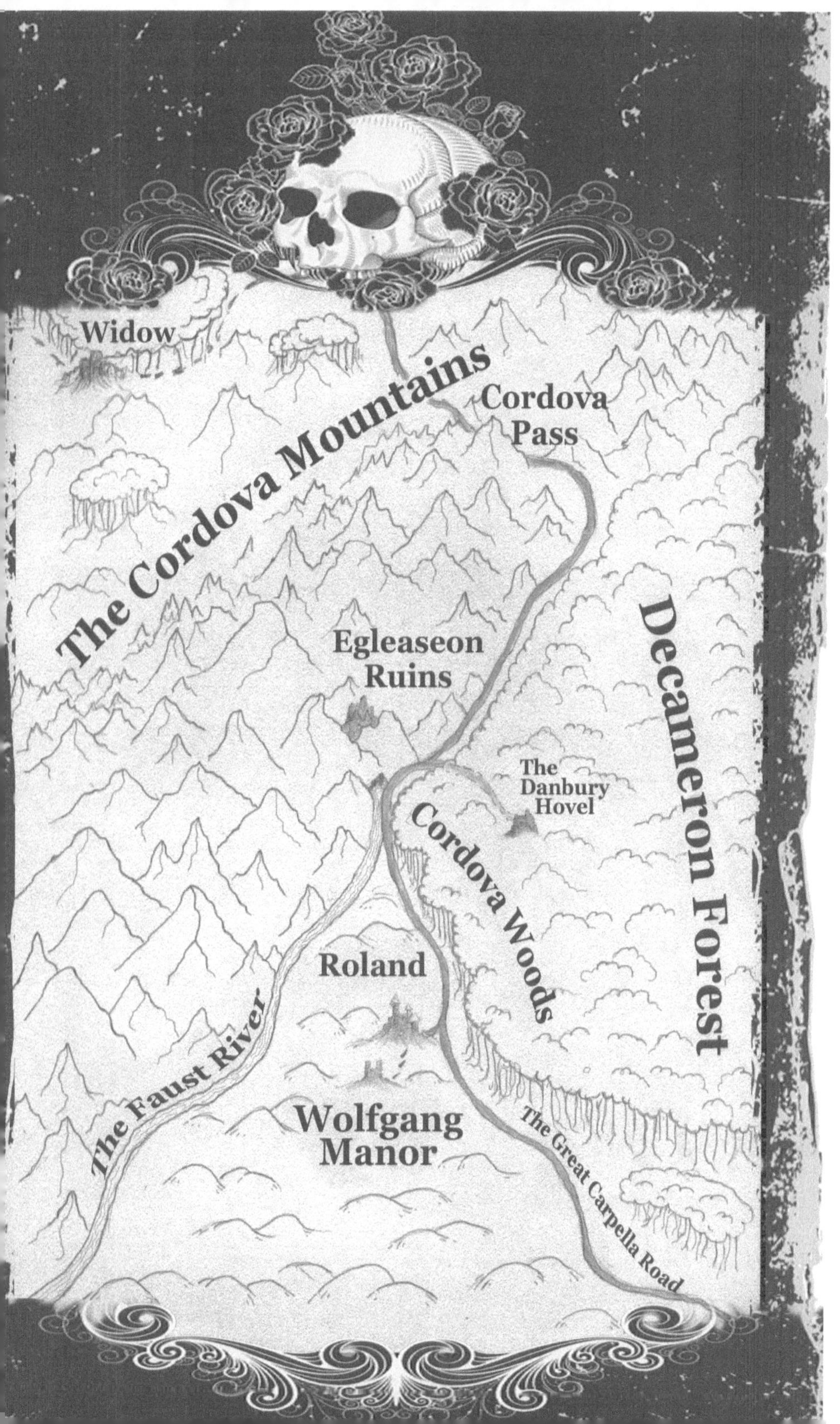

Widow

The Cordova Mountains

Cordova Pass

Egleaseon Ruins

The Danbury Hovel

Decameron Forest

Cordova Woods

Roland

The Faust River

Wolfgang Manor

The Great Carpella Road

PROLOGUE

EGLEASEON

A LOUD, THUNDEROUS ECHO PULLS me from my thoughts. The huge wooden door vibrates the sconces on the walls in its closing, knocking candles to the floor.

I speak in an ominous tone. "My guest of honor. You have finally come. I take it you met the inhabitants of my castle. I'm sure it was a warm welcome." Sitting on my throne, I stare at the spectacle before me at the bottom of the stairs. A man covered in blood. Someone who has been through battle. There is no doubt the guardians of my castle are dead.

I cannot see his face. A long black cloak drapes over his head and broad shoulders, covering the expensive clothing beneath. A black and red tunic trimmed with gold studs. A mirrored black belt lined with blood soaked stakes. The shirt, from the hips down, drapes over black leather pants. They tuck into a set of tall buckled boots. Despite the dark color, its sheen reflects in the growing dawn. But it's not the color that makes my guest eccentric, it's the massive white cross on his chest that contrasts with everything.

Clenched in his left hand is a strange-looking contraption. A weapon with four straight blades extending from the center handle. The Bawaka blade. Its metal serrated edges drip with red liquid. I have seen it before during our laborious quarrels.

My guest remains near the door transfixed in silence, neither moving forward nor looking around. He is staring straight at me. Staring at the smile on my face.

I clap my hands as I slowly rise from my throne. I want to commemorate him for being the first person to make it through my abode, unscathed and intact. I am no longer bored, so I laugh. "Welcome to my home, Tenor Alvadine Wolfgang."

The man says nothing as he draws back his hood, revealing his luscious golden locks falling around his shoulders. Such a pretty color, his crystal blue eyes are. So menacing. So innocent. He is calm and collected, standing there across the room. He does not move.

There is undeniable tension in the room. But it is neither him nor I who breaks it. There is a sudden breeze and the flapping of curtains.

A terrible cry bellows from the shadows of the chamber. The voice is fierce with the intensity of a gale wind.

"You!" comes the breath of a woman as she lashes out at Wolfgang like a torrent of endless serpents. A dark mass ascends through the air with ferocity, striking with black hands and trailing smoke. Gathering clouds of mist take the shape of a human with claws. Long twisted nails large enough to skewer a horse.

As I watch, there is no delay from Wolfgang. He moves with superb skill between shadow and light. For every blow the woman attacks with, he evades with precision. It lasts only a moment before she moves faster, avoiding the approaching dawn's light.

Like time standing still, the woman attacks faster than the human eye, but Wolfgang holds his own. She strikes at his abdomen and he buckles forward. She swipes at his head and he ducks. Every attack he parries or dodges. His evasions match the woman, both in skill and speed.

She stops in midair suddenly. "Wolfgang! You dare come to my home after what you've done? Such nerves you possess! Such dishonor! You shall pay for your crime, human!"

Wolfgang unfastens his cloak and tosses it into the air behind him. His hand goes to one of the stakes on his belt, drawing it with great speed. With both hands he forms his two weapons into a cross.

"Stop this madness, Katrina!" says Wolfgang, strong and resolute. "I come in peace. There is an agreement between your father and me." He glances over suddenly, as if expecting me to take action. But he has no idea. I am thoroughly entertained.

Instead, I drink from my goblet. I never stop grinning as the cold red liquid touches my lips. My fangs grow long and my face turns dark.

"Bastard," Wolfgang says in a curt manner.

Katrina rushes forward, engulfing Wolfgang with her dark mist, slashing at him with demonic fury. Her hands dance, slicing flesh and spilling blood. I hear pain escaping his lips, but somehow, he manages to remain standing. What heart! What resilience!

Wolfgang retaliates with his blade, cutting at the mist. Every slice separates the smoke and Katrina laughs. She strikes at him over and over, driving Wolfgang into submission. Soon, he is not moving at all. He is staring at something amidst the chaos. Katrina's speed increases, circling around him like a cyclone, a death whirlwind. She continues to spin around and around until she is merely a blur. Wolfgang doesn't move an inch. What is he doing? Then I realize. He is waiting.

Wolfgang thrusts his wooden stake forward, impaling Katrina. No warning. No anticipation.

A loud cry escapes her lips. Her movement is held fast. The long stake is protruding from her heart. I see terror in Katrina's eyes. Her pride. Her glory. All of it is gone now. I hope you learned your lesson, my dearest Katrina.

With a quick motion, Wolfgang severs her head. It falls to the floor and rolls the length of the stairs, one bloody step at a time. Her body collapses into a heap of lifeless flesh.

Wolfgang is breathing heavily. He looks up at me, yet I remain sitting on my throne. Poor soul. He is confused.

I raise my hand in earnest. "Before you accuse me of breaking my honor, know it well that I would never do such a thing. I have existed too long for such trivial nonsense. My daughter acted of her own will. Her fate was her choosing and she chose noncompliance."

Wolfgang looks around the room. "Noncompliance?"

"Yes, my guest. Noncompliance. You should learn it well. When the need to kill becomes too great, the will becomes compromised. The bloodlust renders the conscious beast useless. Even I, her maker, could not subdue the urges she had for you. Her anger, built over time over you killing her brother, transgressed well beyond reason. It was only a matter of time before she snapped. The curse always wins in the end. My deepest apologies."

"I'm not sure I believe you," says Wolfgang, holding his weapons close.

"Clearly."

With the light of the sun filling the chamber, my power is waning. It gleams off my skin, as if any moment my skin would catch fire and evaporate. Wolfgang watches me intently.

"I see the rumors are true. You can walk in the daylight."

"With pride," I grunt, as if he needed proof. "There is no other who can." My eyes begin to flutter. The sun is draining me considerably. I need more blood if I'm going to continue this conversation.

"I believe a congratulations is in order," I say, tapping the arm of my chair with dried fingernails.

Wolfgang eyes me suspiciously. "What, for killing your daughter?"

I can't help but laugh. "Hardly not. Come." I motion with my hand and stand up. "A toast." I make my way to the table where I have poured countless goblets of blood. There is a wine bottle set out for Wolfgang too. I am always prepared for the occasion.

Wolfgang smirks. "A toast to your demise."

"To life!" I say, raising my goblet. "Always so cunning." I drink it all down and slam my goblet on the table. "I hear you and the lovely Diana recently gave birth to a son. A joyous occasion no doubt."

"What do you know of joy, monster? You only know of death and decay. My family is not your concern."

"No," I say with an air of being distraught. "I was hoping to visit you one day once all of this is behind us."

Wolfgang slowly takes a few steps toward me. "Understand this, Egleaseon. No matter what God has in store for you, you will never set foot near my family. As soon as this is over, you are leaving the realm and never coming back."

I smile. "Well then, seems the formalities are over with." I gesture with my hand. "Shall we proceed?"

Wolfgang nods.

"Good. To the matter at hand then. The relic, if you would." Bracing the wooden surface with my arms, I lean forward, holding back my excitement. I have waited for this for so long, and now, here is the man who hated me the most, delivering me the very thing I wanted most.

Wolfgang takes a few steps forward and stops; his crystal blue eyes sparkle in the sunlight. "For two thousand years you've reigned supreme lord over your kind. For centuries you oppressed the people of Roland, brought death and suffering into their hearts. We have fought hand to hand, tooth and nail. And lost the ones we loved. I gladly give you this relic."

Wolfgang reaches behind his back and produces an object wrapped in brown cloth. As he removes the fabric, my blood begins to pump feverishly. It is the size of two closed fists side by side. With two metal bars bound together by sharp barbed wire, shafts of light glint from its metallic surface. Its presence is unnerving. I want to run from it, as far and fast as I can. But I subdue the urges. This is not what I expected.

Wolfgang holds it before him like fragile glass. "The Hand of God."

My eyes are locked on the relic. "What do you know of suffering?" I snap, looking into his eyes suddenly. "I am the only one who knows true suffering and it will come to an end. I cast immortality to the dogs of hell. They can have it, for I seek new life. To be human again. I shed my everlasting curse!"

Extending my hand, I beckon the Hand of God to me. It flies into my pale hand, unchallenged. Its surface is vibrant and warm to the touch. Its energy seeps through my skin and spreads through my body, bathing me in white light. The sensation is unlike anything I've ever felt before. It is terrifying and wonderful all the same. I grab it with my other hand and pull it close to my chest. Yes. Life. I accept you. It pours into my veins, which accept agony, accept the woes of man, accept pain, accept emotion. Accepting all these things. It is all there. Existence. The breath in my lungs is hot. The air is salty. It is all around me.

Looking at my hands, I see they are no longer pale blue but rosy pink. Rushing with living blood. The veins throbbing underneath my skin bulge with certainty. My hair is thick and my skin is moist. I am suddenly very aware of my surroundings in a way I was destined to forget over two thousand years. Yes. I am alive. I am rejuvenated. And I am mortal.

Looking up, Wolfgang is staring at me. Surprise and disbelief riddle his face. He carries the visage of absolute denial. I am changed and I am immediately aware of the absent powers I once commanded. I attempt to call the fire, the shadow, but it doesn't come. I take a deep breath and exhale. It does not matter. I am free of my earth-bound prison and now death is a force to reckon with.

And so it happens.

Before I take my first step, before I speak my first word, my body is struck with a heavy weight. I was certain I'd have more time, but it comes without warning. An unbearable crushing force, pushing the air from my lungs and compressing my head in agonizing pain. I do not recall ever feeling pain like this before. I try to move, but it's useless. I see Wolfgang slowly stepping away from me, hand on his weapon. A cautious look betrays his face. He is terrified of me.

Then the memories begin consuming me. One by one.

All the murders I've committed. All the sacrifices I've gone through with. They rip at my skin and crush my bones. The centuries catch up to me. Screams of children wail in my ear. God's punishment, yet I do not bend.

My body dwindles away to nothing. Raising my arms, I watch the flakes of my skin peel away and the muscles uncoil from my bones. Soon I am merely a skeletal frame with the consciousness of a man. In the next few moments I will become dust. This is not the end. I look upon Wolfgang one last time and smile.

SIXTEEN YEARS
LATER...

I LOVE MY FAMILY. I would do anything for them. They are what keep me together in this hell of a world. They are why I do the things I do, see the places I've seen, and never speak of the horrors my eyes witness . . .

DAY ONE

WOLFGANG

CHAPTER
I

BENT OVER MY DESK, FEATHER in hand, I look out my study window to see my son practicing against wood and straw. He is excellent with a sword and at his best times, can outdo me with a pair of them. Down in the courtyard his footfalls shuffle masterfully about, kicking up dust as his extended hands balance the rest of his body to keep from spilling over into the mud. With a flick of his wrist, the sword flies from his hand. A pumpkin resting atop a wooden post is reduced to squash. An excellent move. He learned that from me.

Other than possessing the same golden hair as mine, I can't help notice how much he looks like his mother. Dark eyes. Slim narrow face. All of it ending with a curled lip. Sweat drips from his brow as his hair whips about. Yes, so much the same. So much like Diana. My wife. She comes now to meet him. Her long hair flowing behind her, tossed about in its dark waves of ebony. Glass pitcher in hand, she pours Dorian a drink. They pause for a moment from their conversation and turn to see me up in my window. They wave. I wave back.

My sun and moon. Angels sent from God. How I yearn to be with them all the time.

But rarely is there time for pleasurable things. I am always on the quest, the hunt, and today is no exception. Already, Joachim is rapping on my study door. I take what little repose I have left of my quiet morning, and gaze at the brown spider spinning its web round and round in the corner, just where the crook meets the hinge of the frame. How simple life is for that spider, threading away, undisturbed. Simple yes, but meaningless. I can't afford meaningless. Not when there is so much work to be done, so much killing.

"Enter."

Joachim enters into my sanctuary. His dark grey eyes stare into mine before glancing at the tray he holds in his hands. "Morning black for your breakfast, sir, and this"—he points at a yellow envelope sealed with red wax—"has just arrived this morning. The courier man seemed most ecstatic with its delivery. He said it was something along the lines of urgent."

I can never tell if Joachim is happy. His sarcasm hides everything.

I gather the letter almost instantly, forgetting the need for caffeine. "Please, Joachim, set it there. That will be all for now." Quickly I break the familiar seal with my desk knife to unveil the letter of distress. Red wax, yellow sleeve, the mark of an attack. My eyes pass along the print and immediately I come to the realization that today I will be more distraught than usual.

Joachim is already on his way out when I forbid him to leave. "Joachim, wait. Inform Kronklich to ready the coach with double runners. We will need to make great haste where we are going. Provisions for a full day's outing, too."

Turning his head to the side, Joachim pauses in the door-frame. "Yes sir, dutifully so. Shall I summon your wife and son to meet with you in the foyer?"

I hesitate. I always do. Diana and Dorian know what I do; they have for a very long time, and my son strives to be much like his father. But to see the worry in their eyes when I leave pains me so.

"Yes, have them meet me, I will be down soon." I move to the far wall of my study as I hear Joachim close the door behind him. Between rows and rows of bookcases sits my wooden chest. Its contents are what I need today. Creaking the lid open, I bend an arm. With a slight grunt, I heft my leather-plated harness from the trunk and lay it across my workbench, admiring the large white cross stitched upon its surface. Compliments of my wife. Next I retrieve three wooden stakes, a catch of holy water, and my most cherished weapon, the Bawaka, consisting of four straight blades symmetrically laid out to form an X. Bound in dark leather, the handle allows the weapon to be gripped at the center from any angle. The Bawaka is fiercely sharp and precise. Having been passed down through the many generations of the House of Wolfgang, its origin is unknown to me.

I lay everything down next to my proofing, admiring the collection before me, stained from years of victims. I run my hand over the hard leather, feeling the dried glue over holes where monster teeth once were. Placing it over my body, I pull each thong of leather through its buckle.

Stopping in front of the oblong mirror, I check all my straps once more before leaving. Pushing aside a pale lock of hair, I see the sagging under my eyes. Sleep was anything but my friend last night. How many hours of the night passed while I stared at the tick of the clock? I reach for my abandoned morning black as I make my way down to the foyer.

Passing through the long corridors of my manor, I admire the immense collection of artifacts obtained over the years. The Axe of Fallon. The Solstice Cup. Horn of the Minotaur. Every time I pass this way, I am flooded with memories, the deeds I've done, the beasts I've slain. It strengthens me, injecting me with new hope that one day my efforts will finally come to an end, that the village of Roland will know true peace once and for all.

I reach the end of the stretch and descend the stairwell, passing tapestry after tapestry, sewn with reds, blacks, and whites, honoring the colors of my house, a family pride dating back centuries ago.

Diana and Dorian await me at the bottom, standing brighter than any stars. They are full of smiles, until they see my descent. Leather creaking on my back, blade swaying on my hip.

My own smile is genuine, but it is not enough to thwart the dolorous looks I receive.

"Don't worry, my dear, the journey calls for only a day. I will be back before the sun fades red." I speak the truth, but broken promises of the past still linger in her heart.

Diana holds the crystal pitcher in her hands. They tremble as she speaks. "How long will you answer the calls of the helpless, day in and day out, when your family is here, always wondering if you will return from the day's hunt. Curse you, Tenor, you're always gone."

Such are the sweet words of my Diana. Life would not be complete if it weren't for those words, *Curse you, Tenor.* It is her saying that stays my soul. Her way of showing affection when we are not behind closed doors. I smile at her again. "I love you, Diana." She smiles back.

"Father," begins Dorian, his black eyes pierce my soul like his mothers, "You weren't going to leave without saying goodbye?"

I'm about to tell him no, when he interrupts me.

"You will need this." He holds his sword up before me, scabbard and all. A braid of white gold is spun into the pommel of black and red. The weapon of the Wolfgang House. The vampire blood the sword has tasted is countless.

"Not today, son," I say, glancing at him, and then to my wife, "I won't need it. I'm to go to a simple investigation. You hold on to it." I squeeze his shoulder. "You worry me, boy, the way I see you practicing with it. Soon you will be better than me."

A smile fades his look of determination.

"The boy," interrupts Diana, "is just that, a boy. He is not a day older than sixteen and already you coax him to slay monsters. I tell you, Tenor, teaching him to kill so young is not the best idea you've ever come up with. It will spell dangers beyond your grasp." She sets the glass container down on a lamp table, freeing her hands. She comes closer to me, swinging her arms around my neck. The fragrance of her sweet skin, mixed with the oil of my harness, creates the familiar scent of my departure. I step through the foyer toward the door but she keeps stride with me.

"Yes, sixteen now and next year, he will be of age, and become a true Wolfgang. All monsters shall come to fear him, and so will I," I say with a wink.

The sound of a throat clearing turns our attention toward the entrance. Joachim stands motionlessly erect in the opening. His long black hair and crushed velvet coat give him an odd looking appearance against the grey overcast sky. "Pardon for the intrusion, sir. Kronklich demands your audience. He says there is a dire situation afoot." He steps back from the frame of the doorway as he waits for me to pass.

"There, you see, there is nothing to fear. The worst to happen to me while I'm gone lies just beyond that door." My joke about Kronklich softens the stagnant goodbye. Everyone loves Kronklich, everyone except Joachim; the morbid butler dislikes all things, it seems. But Kronklich has been my faithful driver for many years, serving my needs just as well as anyone else with horse and reign. And hardly just a driver. He provides many other professions. Courier. Rancher. Doctor.

I kiss Diana passionately goodbye, feeling her soft warm lips tenderly, the scent of fruit upon her breath. I eye Dorian proudly before embracing him. I address Joachim before my family as I always do. "Be sure to tend to things while I'm gone and keep them safe."

"As always, sir, I shall never sway from my duties." Joachim's grey eyes stare into mine for a brief moment until I finally turn to see my wife and son one last time. I nod and depart through the front door to see a flock of crows vanish into the trees.

CHAPTER
II

THE AIR IS CHILLY FOR late September; it passes through the vents of my harness causing a slight chill to my bone. I will need my coat it seems. Passing through the front yard of the manor, I walk along the three-foot-high walls that have already begun to boast the curling vines of pumpkin and squash. The land around the manor is covered with such various fruits this time of year, accompanied by the turning colors of yellow and brown leaves. The servants of my estate tend to the numerous piles set about the acreage. The men with their brown coats and caps, the women dressed similarly except for the substitution of long skirts.

The carriage is at the end of the stone cobbled drive, waiting to whisk me away. There, I see Kronklich's unusually long top hat, bobbing up and down in a panic. He is inspecting the buggy as if he lost something precious to him. As I approach, he has almost fully inspected the team of mares and the black coach. He starts at my approach, but recovers with uncanny vigilance.

Dressed in one of his finest grey suits—it is the color he insists on wearing—he shakes his head worriedly. "Confounded all to hell, that's what this situation has led me to say! I tell you, when all the bergamot has gone missing, it is a bad day indeed to travel! What with the cool air about and the endless bombardment of foliage, 'tis no wonder that the blackest of tea should be consumed. And yet here I am and there you stand, and not an ounce of bergamot to be passed around."

I am unsure if he is in a stable state when he continues further. "By God's good grace, Lord Wolfgang, here is your coat."

Graciously, I take the long mantle of black and cover myself, welcoming the warmth. I look at Kronklich with slight annoyance. "You know I dislike when you use my proper title in such a way. There is no need, James."

A look of knowing shows on his face. "Indeed, Tenor, indeed you are correct, but I merely prepare for the character that will undoubtedly appear later this day. We can't have civilians seeing your lordship's servants addressing him by first name. T'would be dishonorable."

"Indeed," is all I say as I inspect the cargo.

"You will find that all preparations have been readied," Kronklich replies, a slight hesitation in his delivery.

Satisfied with the walk around, I enter into the coach and lean my head out the window. "Yes, James, it is duly noted, more bergamot for the manor."

A smile of perfectly straight teeth shows his contentedness as he ascends onto the buggy. "Excellent, Lord Wolfgang," and he cracks the whip, sending the black carriage into speedy departure.

I nearly lose my head from the sudden jolt and retreat back into the stuffy interior. The wind whips my hair about as we take flight down the avenue of tall conifer trees, which reach as high as the lowest clouds. A quick turn at the drive's end and we are no longer on my estate. Into the village of Roland we go. It's a good day, with the air crisp and the villagers working outside looking productive. The hustle and bustle will continue till the beginning of winter, for when the cold snow comes off the Cordova Mountains to the north, there will be no more passage out of the valley. The quaint town of Roland will settle in for its hibernation, and those who do not prepare for the solstice will suffer like they always do.

Pothole after pothole we descend into town; the clatter of hooves upturn pebbles from the cracks of the cobbles. We pass shacks, houses, and other mansions, reaching the base of the town, its center the deepest dip in the valley, then the long climb back up through the moist streets. We see Albestan Church on the right, with its lofty priests tending to the roadside wash of passing buggies. The might of the holy cross sits proudly just below the nape of the triangular shaped roof, a symbol to all that sanctuary awaits for those inside chased by demons. It's a place to visit the choir and share one's earnings.

Another pothole returns my mind to the inside of the carriage and I see that Kronklich has come far more prepared than anticipated. I open a trunk that lies underneath the opposite seat. Inside lie all the necessary tools for any unfortunate circumstance: wooden stakes and holy water, enough to take on a brigade of vampires.

My hair dashes about wildly as I lean my head out the window. The air stings my watery eyes. I shout to Kronklich, "Are you anticipating something I'm not aware of?"

He smiles back at me, keeping his focus on the road. "Nothing out of the ordinary, sir!" A quick snap of the reigns and the carriage lurches again. I fear he is going to snap my neck.

Almost out of the village now, the increasing onset of trees comes forward quickly and the buildings decline just as fast. Out of civilization, we speed into the gloom of the surrounding woods, following the Great Carpella Road. The sun is near its midday travel by the time Kronklich slows the pace of the horses. Somewhere, through the foothills of Cordova, along the outskirts of Roland is our destination. A hovel, lost and forgotten, which few inhabit. For another hour we bounce along the dirt road, the potholes now replaced with roots and rocks. Off in the distance, above the tree line, I make out the faint shadowy remains of Egleaseon Castle, a memory I still hold vivid to this day. I went there by personal invitation from Egleaseon himself, lord of the vampires, to deliver him the one item that all vampires fear most: The Hand of God. A relic so powerful, it has the ability to revert a vampire back to its original human form by the mere touch of it. But Egleaseon did not fear it. In fact, he embraced it. He wanted to become human again and when he took the Hand of God from me, something unexpected happened. All the time he lived as an immortal vampire aged him within seconds. Did he know this? I'm not quite sure. In the brief moments following, he was rendered to dust. I watched his ashes scatter across the castle floor and barely escaped with my life. The whole castle came down in crumbling demise. Even to this day I try to make sense of his suicide, but can't.

There is the familiar sound of "Whoa, good lads!" as the carriage is brought to a sliding halt. Kronklich is always trying to impress with his superb driving skills. Looking out of the window, I see a dark forest in all directions, but no place of destination. I make to lean my head out of the window to question our sudden pause when something catches the corner of my eye. An enormous spider. Larger than two hands side by side, it makes its way along the headboard. Its silvery hair brushes along the wood, shuffling and scraping. Suddenly it's flattened by a wooden cane. Kronklich's face appears in the window. He no longer smiles.

"We have arrived at the Danbury Hovel, Lord Wolfgang," he says in a clear, distinct voice.

I step out into the shade, as the scarce sunlight dodges between the trees. I make my way along the soft earth to a beaten down cottage, initially blocked from my line of sight by the horses. The smell of death lingers in the air. Kronklich is mere steps behind me as he follows, his fantastic suit a severe contrast to the surroundings. He carries his long cane with him while speaking about the cottage just yards ahead of us. "Not too bad. I've seen worse."

"As have I." My eyes scan the area and there is movement to the left. A small gathering of people huddle together, all of them appearing quite nasty, some covered in mud, others in blood. Among them stand two adults and four children, most likely relatives of the victimized woman inside. I hear them whimpering in the distance, shaking their heads, holding their ears. One of the adults holds a cross in his hand, praying. I can only imagine what they saw last night.

I motion with my head in their direction. "You know what to do." There are no further words exchanged between us, for Kronklich understands his role. Too many times we have seen the abomination of such tragedies. The vampires always strike these secluded areas deep within the woods, attacking the innocent, killing children, women, and grown men; it matters not. Those unprepared cannot stop the attacks. That is why I'm here.

I try not to pay attention to the adults talking with Kronklich. Their words are full of dread and sorrow. I focus on the house before me instead, taking in its worn appearance: a door, a window, not much more. There is nothing that appears unusual, except for the huge spider infestation that seems to have taken over the corners of the front room. The silver spiders are all over the woods. I've heard tale they are harmless, but who's to say that their numbers can't overrun. Stepping up to the door, the children are whimpering louder than before. I wonder if they weep for their dead mother or harbor worries for my own sake. There is no doubt those children have heard of me; this isn't the first time I've been around these parts.

I attempt to test the handle to see if it's locked, but there is no handle. Dozens of silver spiders crawl along the horrible thatching of the roof. With my mantel comfortably covering my shoulders and weapons, I pull the makeshift door of planked wood open, letting the dust take its course. Mold and the stench of death fill my nostrils as I stoop through the low opening.

The small room is dark and full of smoke. There are beams of light seeping through the window. From what I can deduce, the hearth lies on the other side of the room and its smoke smothers everything with its noxious fumes. I pull the collar of my mantel over my nose and mouth, attempting to squelch the desperate urge to cough. Immediately, my eyes fall upon a lifeless figure on the floor by the only table in the common room. It is too dark to tell if it is a man or a woman so I assume it's the woman I'm looking for. As I approach slowly, I keep a mental note of my surroundings: Scattered barrels, two chairs, and a large pile of straw that is stained a dark brown.

Standing above the body, the usual scent comes from it—not the death that normally comes from human remains, but the stench of cloves and burnt leaves. The undead. Instinctively, my hand grips the wooden stake on my belt as I kneel to turn her over. The corpse turns with ease. Rigor mortis has not set in yet. Another sign of what I must do, and soon. But for final confirmation, I move a lock of the woman's hair away from her neck, exposing what I have already calculated.

Two puncture wounds along her milk white skin.

I say a soft prayer over her forehead while I slip one of God's instruments from my belt. "I release you from your infernal bonds." Just as quick as the words flow from my tongue, I drive the wood deep into her heart. Her eyes open wide with the familiar pain I have dealt so many times. A gasp escapes as she passes on to true death. She tries to raise her head from the ground, but my hand firmly keeps it down. "Go now, woman. Pass on to God. Be with him now."

Her body goes limp.

A door from another part of the room flings open as something runs straight for me. It screeches a fearful cry, and I have no time to react. The child clings to me as if I were his father, sweating and covered in grime. He cries and cries hysterically, shouting incoherently. I do my best to calm the boy, but he keeps looking at his dead mother. Had he been in the closet hiding all this time? Seems there were five children, not four. And as his tears finally begin to let up, I notice a place on his neck he covers with his hand. Blood trails from underneath and I am left with dread of the worst kind.

"My mum. My mum," says the boy as I move his hand away from two holes, similar to the ones in his mother's neck.

Holding the slippery stake, a moment passes and I know that I cannot do it. He is just a boy and suddenly I am thinking of Dorian. Could I drive a stake through a boy who reminded me so much of my son? Little blonde curls, large dark eyes. The boy seems the same age when Dorian performed one of his first plays. So young. So innocent. I have only seen a child turned vampire once before. I couldn't kill it then and won't do it now. I rise from the floor and make to leave, shivering, leaving the little vampire to his perished mother.

Muttering deliriously to himself, he suddenly calls out after me. "Please, mister. Please, help me. Are you going to leave me?"

I say nothing as I pass out into the daylight, knowing the boy cannot follow. Outside, Kronklich is having a difficult time detaining one of the four children. Walking slowly back to the carriage, I see the girl running over to me, her long braids of golden hair matted down with filth. Kronklich chases after her, but it's too late. She grabs my arm. Dirt marks her face like a homeless child. "Mr. Wolfgang, sir, please, what of our mother?"

I have no words for her as I look into her hazel eyes. I see the unmistakable fear of helplessness and unknowing, the doubt that ebbs in all humans. I grip her shoulders just like I would with Dorian. "Please, see to your brothers and sisters. They need you now."

I turn her away as Kronklich approaches me. "Terribly sorry, Lord Wolfgang, they are quite a handful," he says out of breath.

I look at him sternly, waiting for his full attention. "The others, do they carry any sign?"

He looks back at the bundle of children and then to me. "None."

"Good," I say as I turn around to head for the carriage. "Evil prevails in this house, Kronklich. The vampire will return if it's not purified."

"Yes, of course, Lord Wolfgang."

There is a shout of glee from the girl suddenly. She runs to the cottage's only window yelling with joy. "Michael! It's Michael, look, he's alive!"

It is so much harder knowing their names.

I eye Kronklich sternly. "Get her out of there. And Kronklich," I say, pausing for a moment, as he looks at me with unease, "make it quick."

It is now late afternoon and the sun has ducked behind the hills. As he pulls her away from the window, I see Michael staring at his brothers and sisters through the windowpane. Sorrow besets his face. I can only imagine what the little man is thinking. His gaze turns to me and I look away.

CHAPTER

III

As I sit waiting in the seclusion of my carriage interior, I smell the smoke filling the woods. Too soon I hear the horrific cries of Michael's family as they watch their brother burn with their home, their mother, and all that they know. Why am I so weak?

With the jostling of the carriage, I know Kronklich is back aboard his post. A quick snap of the reigns signifies our departure. In time, the smoke clears and the ride returns to normalcy. I watch the trees stream by quickly as neither Kronklich nor myself speak. The sun is well on its descent by the time we come to rest the horses for a bit. We are at a crossroads where merchants have set up their wares. I remain in the coach pondering in silence the horrors that were committed earlier. I imagine the boy biting his mother's neck while she was holding him close. Such a disturbing thought.

A pair of yellow moths flutters by in the nearby wood, Diana's favorite. Kronklich comes back moments later holding a few bags of herbs, shaking them with pride down below at me. "Pure bergamot from the hills of Ashton."

He takes my silence as a sign to press on.

When the day lingers, the sky slowly changes color. Unlike other investigations, today was exceptionally taxing on the mind. The letter mentioned nothing of children.

The carriage takes a hard left and soon, we are out of Cordova Woods and back on the Great Carpella Road where I see the darkening clouds of the approaching night. But the sunset itself is beautiful as I jostle about the carriage; what wonderful pastel colors the sky makes, from yellows to orange, and now to pink, cascading to purple, and now to red. I pause a moment and realize something isn't right.

I stick my head out as far as I can from the carriage window, straining my neck in an awkward angle. "James, do you see that?" Just as I finish the question, I look up to see Kronklich loading a crossbow with one hand.

"Indeed I do, sir," he says, putting down the weapon and grabbing a second one.

Again I look off toward the horizon and my speculation is correct.

The village of Roland is ablaze.

"Don't stop the carriage," I say as I grip the edge of the window and hoist myself onto the post next to Kronklich. He is not fazed. "I'll take over driving, you just keep loading."

With reigns in hand, I lash out hard, commanding the pair of mares to go faster. Froth drizzles from their mouths. Their nozzles mist with moisture. Without mercy, we descend into the valley at lightning speed, catching the occasional rock with bone-jarring force. I hear the tension on the wooden wheels, the bearings rattling in their sockets.

Already in the distance, I hear the raging fright of the villagers rising into the night, their wails ghastly, and then slowly, one by one, pair by pair, we pass villagers running for their lives. There is no time to stop and ask questions. I dodge a man running straight for the carriage, delirious and terrorized, flailing his arms about his face.

We pass Albestan Church, avoiding as many potholes and fires as possible. Kronklich nearly falls from the post. I grab his expensive suit tearing one of his sleeves. Straight ahead of us, monsters crowd the streets. Bogarts, with their sharp claws and papery skin. Caretakers, with their skeletal bodies and swinging lamps. They raze the town, pummeling villagers into the ground, trampling them with their bones and claws. Everything is chaos.

Kronklich fires off a shot, piercing a bogart's face, splitting its one eyeball in two. He sets the crossbow down and readies the next.

The thought of reaching my family makes me frantic; I crack the whip harder, demanding absolute obedience from my horses. The carriage barrels straight into a crowd of caretakers, smashing their bones into a storm of shrapnel. Wheels grind over the remains as Kronklich hurriedly tosses bones from the post.

My cloak flaps in the rush of the wind, cracking as loud as the reigns. Focusing on not overturning the carriage, my eyes lock only on the dim outline of the road ahead. I hear Kronklich shouting in my ear. "They're aboard!" he says, but I dare not look. He vanishes from my side for too long and I chance glancing back. He is gone. There is no time to ponder. He would tell me to keep going. I crack the whip harder. I see Wolfgang manor in the distance through the smoke. My pulse quickens when I see it's on fire. Flames rise high from the rooftop.

A hand grasps my wrist suddenly and the team of horses veers from the road missing a ditch. It is all I can do to steer the carriage true while pulling Kronklich back onto the post.

We are at the avenue of tall conifers racing along its path and everything is a blur. We don't stop till we're at the head of the long drive into the entrance. Bodies of my servants are strewn about. Arms torn from limbs. Necks raked open. All of the pumpkins and squash are smashed; the front door, splintered into a thousand pieces.

Jumping down from the carriage, I run, discarding my long mantel for better movement. The chill of the night stabs my bones, but my adrenaline rushes from my heart and keeps me warm. Kronklich follows suit, strapping a crossbow over his shoulder and carrying another in his hands. Without his top hat, and with his hair all askew, his appearance is that of a mad scientist.

We pass into the shadow of the house, covering each other. The smoke is thick inside, but no visible flames have penetrated the main part of the house. I pull the Bawaka blade from my hip as I step over two servants. Their faces have been ravaged. Gore covers the walls.

Room by room we search for signs of Dorian and Diana. Upstairs and down. But there is no sign of either. Just as I begin to ascend the steps for a second look, Kronklich grabs my shoulder. "Out there! Look!"

Through one of the windows overlooking the back courtyard, I see my wife lying in the dirt in the same spot where she stood with my son this morning.

I run for the nearest door.

Bursting into the courtyard, I stumble past more bodies and fall to the earth before her. Fire rages all around in the hay, the rooftops, and the second floors. Tears stream across my face as I hold my hands before her, deciding how to go about examining her. Her clothes are disheveled and blood cakes her fingernails. I reach to her neck and wait. Her skin is cool to the touch, but a pulse resonates from within. Dear God, she's alive!

I cradle her body into my arms, hugging her ever so close to me, feeling what warmth is left. She is slowly slipping away into the cold night. Her breath is shallow. I barely make out the words she whispers into my ear. Oh, her sweet breath! Diana! I listen as best as I can. She stammers words that do not make sense.

"I cannot stay here, my love. I must go."

"Diana! No, you are delirious, my dear. Stay with me. Everything will be all right. I promise." I grip her tighter in my arms as if to prevent her spirit from leaking into the night.

"Curse you, Tenor, I will always love you."

Those are her last words before she is gone.

"Diana. Diana! Don't do this to me. Don't leave me—please—" My tears become sobs as I gently place her limp body down. Her skin is so pale. A bluish white. A thought enters my mind, much like when I was in the cottage with the boy. I turn her head to see the other side of her neck and I tremble.

She has been bitten.

I sit lost in the haze, staring into the heavens above, then at the fire raging all around me. Gently I place Diana's arms to her side, and push the strands of hair from her face. She looks so peaceful, but I know when first light comes, she will rise to the horrors of evil. This last act as her husband I must do, it is all I can do, and I curse the night for allowing evil to prevail here.

Pulling a wooden stake from my belt, I grip it with both hands and raise it above me. I scream into the heavens for absolution and drive the holy wedge deep into the heart of my loving wife. Despite her cold flesh, her blood is warm as it spurts onto my face and hands. Her blood, so nurturing . . . the very blood that gave life to my son. I hear the last gasp of earthly dwelling escape her lungs, and I know that it is over.

With tears still dripping from my chin, I stand before her ravaged body to say goodbye for the last time. She will stay here and burn with the evil that has befallen Wolfgang Manor.

When Kronklich approaches, he does his best to avoid my eyes as I turn away. "Kronklich, there is much work to be done. Salvage what supplies you can."

Already the manor has turned into a blazing inferno and there isn't much time to prepare.

Disjointed thoughts race through my brain as we pack the carriage with rations of food. Thoughts of my son and Joachim. I can see nothing to indicate their whereabouts. Where did they go?

Alive or dead. I need to find them.

There are wisps of smoke smoldering on Kronklich's suit from the heat of the manor. He leans against the carriage, taking deep breaths. "Tenor, what will we do now?"

I take a moment looking at him with gratitude and then turn to watch Wolfgang Manor cave in on itself. The night sky is lit with sparks and bits of the fallen building. We both witness the sight in awe at the sheer power of the element. But in the next moment I force myself to snap my thoughts together. Kronklich has done so much for me. I couldn't ask for a better servant. No. A better partner.

"We need to find answers," I mutter, motioning for him to follow me. "And we won't find them here."

CHAPTER IV

I AM A MAN OF my word. Even now, as I explain my plans to Kronklich, the look of confusion besetting his face shows doubt.

"But Tenor, what you're saying is madness. Is it even possible?" Kronklich looks at me with those terrible eyes, the eyes of a hawk, inquisitive, ready to dissect me.

"Maybe," I say. The day's events have taken their toll on my body. I am tired, but determination pushes me forward. "We must return to the village, see Father Bronin."

I cough from the smoke lingering in the air as I enter the buggy. For the first time in months, I am grateful for its comfort. Soft plush seats of red velvet. With my back against the opposite door, I watch the remaining flames of my home burn into the sky. Already I am plagued by the images in my head. My beautiful Diana. Her body burning away in the fire as I left her dead in the dirt. Her face crumbling to ash. I try to make sense of what happened, but sense has eluded me. Dorian, my son, and

Joachim, my servant, are missing. I try to distract my mind, but it is impossible.

I smell Diana's blood all over my hands and leather proofing. I begin to sob. I don't care if Kronklich hears. The pain is uncontrollable. My whole family, torn asunder in a night.

The crack of the whip sends the carriage into motion, shaking my senses. The conifers along the gravel road pass by as looming shadows in the sky. With the moon only half full, the limited light conceals the massacred bodies of the dead servants out in the field.

Eventually, my tears dry as red rivers across my face. I feel the caked blood and salt stiffen within the folds of my neck. The carriage ride is a temporary reprieve as Kronklich guides us into town. I stare at the lantern as it sways in rhythm with the galloping of the horses, squeaking with each bump. It reminds me of the caretakers, the skeletal frames I saw attacking the people of Roland. Evil souls possessed within bones, hunting for new bodies to claim. Those abominations never come into the town.

"We are nearing Roland, Lord Wolfgang," says Kronklich in his formal address. I'm not sure the etiquette is necessary anymore, but I am too exhausted to argue. We rapidly approach the town, emerging from darkness and into the bright red glow of burning buildings. The smell of smoldering wood and charred flesh stings my nostrils as I glare out the window. A sense of foreboding overcomes me when I see the damage done to Roland. Corpses lie in the street, trees lie broken at the mast, carriages have careened into fences.

Townsfolk wander aimlessly about in shock. Some run to raging fires with spilling buckets. I see a couple, a woman holding her husband, crying over his tortured body. His legs are gone. I could remove myself from the carriage, go to her, comfort her, tell her I too, have suffered the same. But the thought is pointless; she is lost within her own nightmare. Solemnly I observe a little boy pull at his sister's limp body, blood trailing from between her legs. I turn my head in disgust.

What wrong had these people committed to deserve this? Did God abandon them or did I fail in my duty? Deep in my stomach a sudden pain rises with the thought that all of this suffering is because of me. Maybe I, Tenor Alvadine Wolfgang, have somehow upset the natural order of things, slaying the monsters and beasts of the night. Maybe Diana's father was right. Maybe I have gone too far and this is retaliation. Mother Nature's way of restoring balance.

I try to ignore the thought as we pass a dead man crushed by an overturned carriage, his chest ripped open, rats chewing on exposed rib bones.

A hard thump nearly knocks me from my seat. Gripping the handles, I scramble to see what was hit. A man, naked from head to toe, spins around in the street, and then collapses.

"Kronklich," I call out. "You just hit a man."

"It wasn't a man," he shouts from the top of his post. "I assure you he was already dead."

More thumps follow and I brace my body to keep from sliding off the seat again. Instinctively, my hand goes to my Bawaka blade. The carriage comes to a halt and I peer out.

A crowd of people—like crying angels, shout and bang on a nearby gate, calling out God's name for mercy. These must be the townsfolk who survived the onslaught of the vicious monsters. Some are bleeding profusely and others have barely a scratch. For a moment the scene is surreal to me, as if I were in some madhouse of crazed inmates. I look up toward the sky and see a holy cross piercing the night sky. Albestan Church.

The banging becomes louder as the hysterical mob clangs on the wrought-iron gates with shovels and pitchforks. They are seeking help from the church, but the gates are locked tight. A rusted chain prevents their advance. Where were the priests and clergymen? They were all here earlier.

A full-bearded man with axe in hand approaches my carriage. He places his bloody hands on the door and leans into the interior. "Hey look," he shouts, waving his hand to the crowd behind him, and pointing toward our arrival, "Lord Wolfgang is here." Spit flies from his face as he talks. There are cuts all over his cheeks and forehead. "Tell those holy fucks, to let us in. We're going to die out here!" For a moment, I am stunned. His eyes carry the faintest trace of red. The townsfolk seem to catch on to what's happening and surround the carriage. They begin shaking it as if to capsize a landlocked boat. My grip tightens around my blade. Any moment now I will take this man's life.

Kronklich calls from above. "Looks like we're trapped, my lord!"

Is Kronklich being facetious?

I raise my blade to separate the bearded man's hands from my carriage, when suddenly, screams unfold from the crowd.

The townsfolk burst into a panic, trampling one another as bogarts claw their way through flesh and bone. Their muscles are taut and their knobby joints allow them to move quickly. The familiar scent of human blood fills the air.

Suddenly everything is forgotten.

The man with the axe runs to the aid of others, as a woman just beyond my reach is raked by hellish claws. She falls to the earth with her back ripped open and an arm dismembered.

God is not here.

I emerge from the carriage, smashing a bogart's head with the door in the process. Wood splinters but I know Kronklich will fix it later. I descend like a billowing shade, mantle crackling behind me. I stand solitary, defiant in a rain of blood and death. Three bogarts surround me. They are quick, but I am faster. I lodge my four-pointed blade in the first one's decayed mouth. Ooze touches my bare hand, seeping between my knuckles, but it's the current of air behind me I notice. I step to the side, dislodging my blade; the Bawaka breaks free from the bogart's face, spilling watery innards onto my boots. I turn, cutting the other two with a mid-level strike and their abdomens split. There is nothing left to support them and they crumple. Just beyond I see Kronklich firing his crossbow into a bogart's forehead, just above its one and only eye.

I nod to Kronklich, who has assured me the carriage is protected temporarily, so I continue my plan. In this fleeting moment, I am left with the image of Kronklich clubbing a bogart with his cane. Each swing turns his grey suit red.

Now the bogarts are coming from every angle. I dare not look over my shoulder, ignoring the villagers' screams. I hear bones breaking, flesh rending. Dozens of bogarts. They know me and are drawn to me like a moth to lichen. They are servants to the late Egleaseon, the vampire lord I destroyed years ago. Why are they here? Who sent them? I must remain diligent and deliver them from this world.

Making way to the gate of the courtyard, a bogart approaches fast and my hand goes to my blade. The bearded man suddenly appears before me. "Go!" he screams, bringing his axe down on the monster, severing the tendons in its neck, the eyeball bulging from its socket. To think I was going to cut the man's hands off. It's only a matter of time before he will die, so I make the best of his sacrifice and keep running, parrying stained nails and teeth.

As I get closer, I notice something approaching the gate from the other side. A man wrapped in brown robes. It's impossible to tell which clergy member it is, but that's the least of my concerns. He carries a large ring with keys. Their metallic shine reflects the embers of burning buildings. He seems adamant to reach the gate and so I press hard to meet him at the bars.

The odds dwindle in my favor as I slash through more skin. More people die as the bogarts continue their onslaught. For every two I cut down, five more appear. It's impossible to tell their source. Where were they coming from?

A woman lies against the gate as I approach, still twitching with half of her neck missing. Shoving her aside, I check the lock on the bars and pull. The gate holds fast. Jingling keys bring my attention to the brown wrapped figure standing before me. I see only parts of him through the gate, his face wet with perspiration. Short locks of brown. Warm brown eyes. Nester.

As he brings one of the keys to the lock, I grasp his wrist. His sodden face turns white. The look of a student caught in the act of a misdeed.

"No, Nester," I say, giving his hand a firm squeeze. "There are too many. They will flood the gate."

"But my Lord Wolfgang, Father—" The boy nearly drops the keys.

I feel him shaking uncontrollably. "Get a hold of yourself," I say with agitation. Nester stares at me. "Wait for my signal."

A strong grip suddenly overcomes my shoulders and I am forced back. All I smell is the flesh of decay as I am extricated from the gate. I wait patiently as I am dragged across the cobblestones, supine, staring at the red clouds. If it weren't for my proofing, my body would be torn apart. A sagging eye and rotten teeth block the fire in the clouds from my vision. The bogart hovers over me like a vulture ready to pillage a prized carcass. My blade goes up, through its teeth and peeling lips, twisting the Bawaka like a corkscrew and dislodging fragments of skull. No sound comes from its throat as I cast its body aside.

Turning onto my side, I see the bogarts coming from every direction.

I roll to my feet and begin shouting the holy words of God, moving faster and faster away from the gate.

My tactic works.

I draw as much attention to me as possible, yet something isn't right. For a moment, I almost feel God's presence, then as before, the void where God should be is shockingly prominent.

I look to the sky and feel the heat of burning buildings on my face. There are so many bogarts. They swarm around me like bees in a hive. I pray I distract them long enough for the carriage to make it through the gate once it's opened.

The first wave speeds toward me like dawn breaking over the horizon. Single yellow orbs and sinewy bodies. They come at once with unforgiving hatred. I lose sight of the carriage and gate. The mighty cross atop Albestan Church is the only landmark emanating from the sea of monsters.

I begin spinning my blade; letting the four points rotate between each hand, twisting at the wrist.

At first my movements are easy. A long drawn swoop of my arm and a quickstep slices the first wave to the ground. Dust from their papery skin lingers in clouds around me. More come and I feel the tension growing. They come from every direction, every angle. Running. Leaping. The seriousness of the situation reveals itself as I feel my own blood suddenly escape my leg. I pull back the bogart sinking its claws into my leg and lift his head up in front of me. With Bawaka in hand, I pierce its chest, twisting the blades. Bones splinter and I force upward, dislodging the bogart's head. Ooze sprays my face, reminding me of Diana—her blood—so warm and sweet, speckling my face. *My Diana.* The thought of her only increases my rage.

I reach for a bogart clawing at my back. I feel the scratching through the proofing. I swing it over my head and down onto the others. They fall into a clump of flesh and three more replace them. Without a moment's pause I flick the blade away from my body. It spins and curves, severing arms and legs in its flight path. It boomerangs in a large outward loop and begins its return to me.

Temporarily weaponless, I reach for a stake at my hip and drive it into an approaching bogart, piercing upward through its mouth and the front portion of its head. It gurgles, collapsing to the floor as the Bawaka returns to me. For a moment, there is hope, a gap in the sea of monsters. I lunge for it, but instantly I'm intercepted. Somehow, I am overpowered. Maybe it's the sheer number of undead, but I have been outnumbered far worse than this.

Forced to the ground, my head jolts with pain. Although I can't see it, I am bleeding. Wetness soaks my hair. My vision is gone, blackened out from the impact, yet I can hear the bogarts all around, their horrid chattering teeth, the clicking of their jaws. Their breath is enough to make me vomit.

Seems I'm fated to be eaten by bogarts. God has strange ways of working with his tools. It's ironic a vampire hunter is to be slain by these lesser creatures. Fate is cruel.

I try again to remove myself from the ground, but evil holds fast. Diana, my love, Dorian, my son; I have failed you both.

CHAPTER
V

THE CHORD OF A MINOR blares into the night sky, drowning out all other sounds. Like the blare of a trumpet quartet, the chord lingers for a moment before the key changes. It is followed by an explosive change in harmony to disharmony, tonality gone, with the fracturing of sensible structure. The music fills my ears and soaks into my blood, nurturing it, passing through arteries, veins, and capillaries, vibrating along my bones until it reaches every crack and corner of my being. The tone of the organ fills me with new instilled hope.

I still do not open my eyes, yet I listen to the bogarts growl in discomfort. I feel their uneasiness, the trembling in their claws and limbs as they hold me down.

The musical chord changes drastically, transitioning into a steady rhythmic pattern, passing into smooth undertones of deep resonance. Slowly I open my eyes and the bogarts are fleeing before me, passing into the far reaches of alleyways and smoldering structures. Propping myself up, I see Nester struggling with the gate and Kronklich driving the carriage toward the courtyard. An eerie calm fills the grounds between my companions and myself. The smooth tones of organ music pour from Albestan Church. "The Passage of Rites." No. "The Crystalline Holy." No, that is not it either. I cannot discern which song it is, but the sound is familiar. I should have remembered the organ.

I collect myself from the street and stagger from the loss of blood. Making my way to the church gates, I pass fresh carcasses of those who mobbed the gate minutes earlier. The bearded man is among them, face contorted in agony. It was only a matter of time.

Nester comes running to me as he sees my approach. No longer holding his large ring of keys, he dons a pail and cloth for the wounded. His small frame is under me before I can protest, placing my arm over his shoulder. A strong boy he is; loyal to no end and passionate.

"Lord Wolfgang, I tried to tell you," Nester begins, innocence in his eyes.

I raise my hand holding the Bawaka. "Not now, Nester." I grimace with each hobbling step, knowing the pain will subside in the hours to come. Nothing brandy won't fix.

The sound of the creaking gate draws my attention. Kronklich pulls it shut. Still brandishing his crossbow, most of the bolts are gone from the holster. "Seems you are well and in good tidings, Lord Wolfgang. Be assured, sir, your tactics worked perfectly. There's not a scratch on the carriage."

Kronklich hasn't seen the side door yet. "Very good. Hardly due to my efforts." I am aware of the organ music again. It continues to play with less intensity. The notes have reached higher octaves. The music comforts me and I see all around the courtyard the remaining survivors taking rest. Nester has left my side attending the wounded. A woman and her infant graciously accept his tenderness, nursing a tear on her arm. I hear him asking her softly the question that is always asked. His mannerism is full of empathy, but it's not enough to dilute the reaction from the woman. She was bitten and her life would now be forfeited. Pathogens always transfer through the saliva. It would be days before she would transform into a bogart, enough time to grovel before God and repent, beg for forgiveness.

My stomach churns. The thought of God's mercy is lost to me. Mothers taken from children. Innocent people dead. *Where was God?* Reaching into the bucket at my side, I wring a cloth and dab at the claw marks on my leg. The water stings immensely, but helps me forget the pain in my stomach. Kronklich passes in front of me, bearing a torch of red fire. Since there are no other clergy members present, he takes up the task of lighting the barrier lamps. The sound of the organ will not play forever and it is now I wonder who was playing it. Nester is out here helping the wounded.

As I approach Nestor, the woman runs by me, sobbing hysterically, passing through the high stone archway leading into the church. A place I know she will feel safe for the moment and then her realizations will come again. I sigh.

"Nester, where are the other clergy members?" I ask. "And what of the fathers and archbishop?"

Nester's face is spattered with blood. "They have all left, my lord, busy on an errand." He swallows his spit as he explains. "I am the only clergy left to watch the grounds."

"If you are the only groundskeeper left," I point to the ascending stairs of the church, "who is playing that music?"

Nester answers resolutely. "I tried to tell you before. Father Bronin is manning the pipes."

CHAPTER
VI

THE MUSIC FROM THE ORGAN gets louder as I move through the back corridors of Albestan Church. It serves as a guide, flowing through the halls, vibrating the air around me. Thick with power. It entices me to move faster. Kronklich follows behind me obediently.

Torchlight glows off the bare walls of the empty tunnel. Our boots splash in the stagnant water, causing rats and tiny insects to shy away as we pass. The ground dips and rises from years of erosion. Cobwebs make up the majority of the ceiling decor and all the while I wonder how the back end of the church has succumbed to such disarray. Certainly the masses at church pull their fair share in coin.

Turning down another corridor, I enter the ancestral hall. Between every other stone in the wall lies a skull speckled with blood. They are displayed behind iron wrought bars, their jaws agape, teeth missing in some, cracks in all. This is the chamber where devotion of one's own blood is given to those long dead, the ancestral archbishops. I pay no homage to them this time, for my urgency is paramount. Covered in bogart blood, I track filth through the church's most sacred grounds, passing straight into the worship chamber.

Instantly I am greeted with a myriad of colors. Brilliant cascades of orange, blue, and yellow. The colors paint the room through stained glass windows. Light comes from large roaring fires burning on opposite sides of the panes. I shade my eyes from the brightness, and see the woman from earlier, the one who would soon become a bogart. She kneels before a pew, her child on the floor next to her, hands folded. She cries uncontrollably, but her sobs drown in the powerful organ music.

The chamber, larger than all of the other rooms in the church combined, opens into a circular expanse. Candelabras line the center aisle; dried wax extends from the drip plates, cascading off the sides to the floor. Some of the wicks still carry a flame. As the music flows through my blood, there is a sharp change in harmony. The intensity drops into decrescendo, quieting to a level of conversation.

I move toward the figure bending before an endless throne of wood and metal pipes, disappearing into the ceiling above. Pews pass alongside me as I walk down the center. From the corner of my eye, I see Kronklich peering behind statues, pointing his crossbow at the shadows.

As I move closer to the organ player, the music stops suddenly, and the figure stands and turns to face me. Red robes and white gloves. The figure's face is hidden behind a gold mask in the image of a tragic smile. Pain is the first thing that comes to mind. Two thin horns of a stag protrude from the forehead crest, wavy and grooved. They sparkle with glossy sheen, as if wet with water. The light from the stained glass windows mix with the gold to create new colors, colors bent beyond their standard chromatic spheres.

"Praise be to God," says the tall man. The voice resonates deep from behind the mask.

I know the response to follow-up with, but I say nothing. The necessity of formalities is long gone. I replace it with impatience. "Where has everyone gone, Father?"

I sense the man will say nothing, but the deep voice responds. "Lord Wolfgang, let us not forget you stand in the house of God."

The baritone of the voice rattles my bones. I stare him down as he begins to undo the clasps. "I know very well where I stand, Bronin. But God is not currently home."

With the mask off I am left staring at a wrinkled face. Radiant blue eyes stare back at me, defiant and shocked. I know I have offended my life long friend, but what choice do I have? I need answers now and the longer I draw things out, the less chance I have of finding my son.

"Blasphemy is not tolerated here," Bronin says, placing his gloved hands on my shoulders. I can barely feel his touch through my armor. He continues, "Lord Wolfgang, you know very well the order left at sunset. They make way for Cordova Pass as we speak. Once winter sets, there will be no passage in or out of the valley. This you know."

My shoulders stay tense. I feel childish for my abruptness, but cannot stifle my concern. "Why didn't the Archbishop come back to aid his people? And the other priests, clergy, what about them?"

Father Bronin lets out a sigh and tosses the mask onto a nearby pew. "You know how the caravan works, my lord. Once in motion, there is no stopping. The caravan left hours before the attack. The Archbishop will not be returning. No one will be returning. Nester and I are here now. We remain to remind those that God is here. He's watching all of us."

"Watching us?" I ask angrily. I can't stop myself. "Where, out there on the streets covered in blood?" My voice echoes throughout the chamber. His grip falls from me. The woman kneeling at the pew turns her head toward us. "Was He watching over us when the families of this town were shredded like meat?" I ask, raking my hand across my chest. "Where was He, Bronin?" Water wells at the corners of my eyes. Is it from the hatred I feel toward God or remembering my beloved family dead?

Father Bronin stares at me.

I look up at the domed ceiling to prevent tears from running down my face.

I feel a tighter grip on me this time. "What has happened, my son?" There is concern in Bronin's words.

I fall to my knees. Immediately Diana shrouds my thoughts. My love. Dead and cold on her bed of earth. I recall the blood flowing through her veins. Plush lips so soft. Her eyes like black pearls. The mornings of her hair, raven locks, twisting through my fingers. Smooth grooves of her neck attracting my kisses.

Then there were the marks, the small traces of dried blood where the fangs retracted. Her face withered away to bone and teeth, flesh pulled taut, head tossed back, hair brittle like straw. Wind blows me away from her to another image. Dorian. Young. Strong. Brawn in the shoulder. Golden locks of wavy hair, his hand brushing away the curl in his eye, black as coal like his mother's. There is a hand on his shoulder, pale with black nails. A crushed velvet sleeve covers the bony arm providing him comfort and security. *Run*, I hear myself say, but nothing escapes my throat. There is no escape from the man with the grey eyes. He is parched. He must drink, yet there is no water.

I look up at Father Bronin suddenly. My rivers of tears have run their course. "My family has been taken from me," I say clenching the air with bent fingers. "She died by these hands." My body trembles. "I killed my wife, Bronin. Drove the stake through and through. My beloved, my one and only. She has burned away with everything I own. Wolfgang Manor lies in ruin."

There is shock on Bronin's face. I see the priestly sympathy drawn for someone who has suffered greatly. But I know his is genuine. His mouth twitches. "This, this can't be, Tenor. Say it isn't true. Diana was a harmless soul. Why?"

I have no words to say. I am left with my spiraling thoughts of Diana.

"Your son? Where is your son?"

There is a voice behind me.

"He is gone. Vanished upon our arrival." Kronklich's voice draws me from my gloom.

I see the doubtful looks surfacing in Kronklich's face as I stand up.

"Vanished—but what of the butler, what was his name—"

"Joachim," Kronklich quickly follows up, " . . . is missing as well. A coincidence, yes?" The sarcasm in his voice is apparent.

"You don't think—"

"Given his certain past," Kronklich interrupts, "Lord Wolfgang and I can only assume Joachim has abducted his son. To what effect is still unclear."

"God, give us strength," breathes Bronin.

I wonder if God hears him after all the things I've witnessed today.

Kronklich could not be closer to the truth, however. My notions about Joachim are the same. Everyone warned me before, a man of a broken past, serving me in my own house. I had a charitable thought, hiring him to work for me. After all, it was I who saved him from his death.

Years ago, he discovered his mother succumbed to the vampire's bite. During those times, public executions were normal. My word alone was not enough to appease the bloodlust of the town. They had to see it for their own eyes, the mighty hunter, absolving the undead to the higher power. Joachim was a teenager then, coming of age, and he insisted on watching. He wanted to see what the work of a hunter was like, and so he watched me plunge the wood through his mother's heart; the one who gave him life died at the hands of Tenor Wolfgang.

Now with both he and Dorian missing, something deep inside tells me Joachim is responsible for it. Jealousy? Revenge? Is this Joachim's way of getting back at me? Despite what he'll have to say when I find him, I know I will drive my blade straight through his cold heart.

There is momentary silence as the three of us stand there before the massive pipes of the organ and the stained glass of the panes.

"Where would Joachim go with Dorian?" asks Kronklich.

Immediately my eyes fall upon Bronin, as he has done the same. There is an unspeakable understanding. I rake my hand through my hair. "Lord Egleaseon's Castle."

"But it's in ruins," says Kronklich shaking his head. "Of all places, why there?"

"Evil never dies," says Father Bronin, blessing the three of us with his hand gestures. "The image still burns in my mind. The falling castle, the horrors surrounding the grounds. Bogarts and caretakers, all of them sentinels for Egleaseon."

I remember the day the castle fell. Bronin watched over the carriage, keeping evil at bay with holy relics while Kronklich hunted the surrounding woods for willdermen. I had come running down the path covered in dust from the rubble. Even though the castle fell, the grounds remained buried under centuries of old stone; the rocks and dirt of that accursed place retained the evil growing for the last thousand years.

Joachim abducting my son, the attack on the town—my next plan of action becomes very clear to me. "We must make for the ruined castle of Egleaseon."

There is no objection from Kronklich as he nods his head. He turns to leave and I grab his arm. There are blotches of red all over his suit. "Let us rest the night. At dawn we leave."

Kronklich slings his crossbow over his shoulder and smiles. "Then at least a good meal is in order." Quickly he exits, leaving Bronin and me alone.

"You are not really thinking of going back there, are you?" Bronin's eyes are inquisitive. "The evil will have had time to manifest. Things will be waiting for you in the shadows."

Already I am thinking of the preparations needed before heading out in the morning. "What choice is there? I must follow my gut. I must find my son."

Father Bronin stares at me for a moment before nodding his head. "Then I will go with you."

Having him along would help, but I am reluctant to accept his offer. "Who would defend the church if you left? Only priests and the Archbishop can play the organ."

"It is no matter. Nester is quite capable from the sessions I've given him. He will suffice."

There is not much I can say, and I nod my head.

A baby's cry draws my attention. The woman at the pew attempts to silence her son, cradling him in her arms, whispering in his ear.

I know it is time and I motion to Bronin. Standing before the woman, I see how beautiful she is, long brown hair to her waist, all turned loose, most of it in her face. Grey eyes peer from under her mop of hair and she pulls her child closer to her breasts. Bronin stands to the side in a less threatening posture, hands pressed together, head bent.

"What is your name?" I ask her. Her eyes flick up at me, pupils dilated.

"Isabella," she says. Her voice is weak, drained from crying.

"All will be well," I say while stepping forward. She does nothing as I take the boy from her, an infant no larger than both my hands together. His head is hairless and smooth. "What is his name?"

"Manson," she manages to say. She begins to shake.

"A strong name. The church will take good care of him." Without inspecting the child further, I hand him over to Bronin who treats the boy like fragile glass.

Bronin moves to the woman and brushes the hair from her forehead. "Go in peace," he says, passing his hand over her body.

Isabella begins to sob as Bronin carries Manson away. I wait until I hear the sound of the door closing before I tell Isabella she must proceed.

Motioning with my hands, I point to the ancestral chamber that I originally passed through. Her face drains of all its color. I wait patiently as she walks through the threshold, passing from the mass chamber. Inside she kneels before one of the skulls behind the wrought-iron grate. Her back is to me, and she shakes uncontrollably. So many times I have done this. I try to imagine being in her position. Would I react the same? The answer is always no.

Bitten victims of vampires take a day to turn; those bitten by a ghoul, take three. I wish I could give her more time with her son, that she could enjoy the precious time she has left with him, watch him laugh and cry some more, but I cannot run the risk. She might flee with her son, leaving Manson to a far worse fate. Tomorrow I leave and so I have no other choice.

Drawing close behind her, I hear her whimpering and heavy breathing. Her scent is that of sweat and flowers. Her back is to me and I clearly see the dried petals in the folds of her hair. Normally I would ask for final words, but I know she will not speak. She cannot. Her mind is elsewhere and I must release her from that dark place.

Quickly, precisely, I drive the blade from my belt in between the second and third rib of her back, her heart pierced in an instant. I feel her body go limp.

The thoughts of the day have taken their toll on me. The destruction of my family and home. The death of a mother and her son. Now the death of another mother. I heave a heavy sigh and my shoulders slump. At least her son has been spared.

Clutching Isabella's hair with one hand, I sever her head with the Bawaka. Blood sprays onto the ancestral skulls on the wall.

CHAPTER
VII

I LIE AWAKE IN A bed of plush sheets and pillows. Uncertain of how long I've slept; my eyes burn and ache from the lack of sleep. A breeze blows through the open window of the clergy room, the place where I took refuge for the night. It is cool and renewing, drying the sweat from my restlessness.

Moonlight pours through flapping curtains of red and white as I recall the events that took place hours ago. Absolving Isabella from her cursed fate. Pulling Manson from her arms, turning him orphan. Eating mutton stew Kronklich prepared, huddled around a fire in the courtyard, trying to keep warm.

No pleasure in any of it.

Something catches my attention and I turn my tear-stricken face to the side. I sense movement. At first, it seems impossible, but the more I come to a fully wakened state, the more I understand what is happening. Within the satin curtains, a figure moves toward me from across the room. Clothed in grey silk, it hardly touches the ground as it advances. As if it were floating. My heart nearly stops at the sight of Diana, her raven hair gently blowing about her thin shoulders. A wreath of peonies crowns her brow. There is something red trailing from her hairline, but her face betrays nothing of pain. She looks content and ready to speak, but words do not escape her lips.

She advances, mauve petals twirling from her hair, landing on the stone floor. Sitting up on my elbows, I am certain my heart has stopped. I must be dead, here, in the afterlife with my wife. There's no explanation for what I see, and no sooner do I call her name, she is before me, drowning my senses.

I try to speak but her finger on my lips stops me. Bending me to her will, I am overwhelmed by the presence of her absence. Is she real?

"Curse you, Tenor," she says in a low whisper. Yet her smile is intoxicating, her voice, real enough. I can't help myself, I reach out, stroking her hair.

"Diana. My love," I manage to say as my hand trembles.

She reaches forward, cupping her white delicate hands around mine.

"Tenor," she says softly, soothing my soul and delivering me into a reality I know isn't possible. Her grip tightens, like someone suddenly stabbed in the gut. "Find our son, Tenor. Find our son."

There is fear in her voice; I can taste it. It lingers in the air like the smoke of war, burning my lungs with every breath. I pull her close to me and her hair covers my face. Sweet peonies spark my emotions. I want to help her, to save her, but from what? She already died by my hands!

"Yes, my sweet love. I will find our son. I will save him," I whisper. I feel her relax in my arms. The soft silk of her garment brushes against my bare chest. "I am doing everything I can." There is no hiding how I feel at the moment. Lost and wanting. Blood throbs through every inch of my body. She is before me in the flesh. Skin so soft. I kiss her clavicle and the curved bottoms of her breasts. I slip my hand beyond the folds of her garment, tracing my fingers along each rib until I stop at the bony prominence of her hip.

"God, I've missed you," I say as her hand journeys down my abdomen and begins to undo the buckle of my belt.

"Remain diligent," she says, whispering in my ear. Her hot breath intensifies the throbbing. "Find strength in me, Tenor." She grabs me, full length. Her hand is warmer than her breath. Waves of heat pass through my torso. How can this not be real? I am harder than stone.

I kiss her chin, the dimple at the corner of her mouth, the lobe of her ear. I am obsessed and my body gives in. All I hear is heavy breathing. Is it mine or hers?

"When all hope is lost, think of me," she says as her mouth covers mine. For a moment, I have no air to breathe, but the sweet taste of her fills my palate. My heart beats faster from the lack of oxygen and then I can breathe again.

I gasp, yet she doesn't stop. Her tongue traces my esophagus and descends lower to my breastbone, stopping suddenly and sucking the skin till it's dark. I am helpless.

Her hand runs the length of my neck, into my hair, clenching a handful. She pulls hard, forcing my head back, straining it, exposing all of my flesh.

Her lips move to the pulsating vein at my neck and I find myself accepting, yet afraid. Is this what she wants? I would do anything for her.

Something sharp pierces my neck and I scream.

DAY TWO

CHAPTER
VIII

I can't stop screaming. Sitting upright, drenched in sweat, I grope at my neck where the pain was so real moments ago. I feel for marks but there is nothing.

Shouts come from outside. Terrible screams of anguish.

It is no longer dark; the light coming through the window is dim and grey. *How long was I sleeping for?* My lungs burn. Smoke has made its way inside. That's odd. Grabbing my head, I try to make sense of the events that took place only moments ago. An empty void fills my chest, knowing none of it was real. I could feel her and taste her, but there is nothing now. Only her final words linger before our departure for the second time . . . "When all hope is lost, think of me."

I am always thinking of you.

The door to the clergy room explodes into splintered wood. Through it, a bogart stumbles over debris and into the chamber, scouring the room with its yellow eye. Sniffing the air, instantly it looks my way.

It runs straight for me, growling from its frothing mouth. I have no time to react. Half naked, I am left to fend with nothing. The Bawaka is on the stand next to the bed, but the bogart is on me before I can reach it. The monster pounces upon me and tosses me like a helpless marionette. Its teeth snap at my face and I turn at the last moment, avoiding its corrupting disease. It tries again, attempting to maul my face. Rancid fluids spatter my skin and I gag.

With its weight temporarily off balance, I manage to release one of my arms, then the other. My hands find its throat and I squeeze hard as its arms flail in retaliation. It rips sheets and pillows with its claws and soon we are struggling in a mist of feathers. My hands crush its throat and although there is a rush of air, it does not stop. I am covered in wood shavings as its claws rake the headboard like a carpenter whittling wood. The only way to stop it is to pierce the head.

The monster now has the upper hand. It pins my arm, knocking over the nightstand as I try to break free. The Bawaka disappears from sight. Struggling, we fall off the bed, landing on my back, knocking the wind from my lungs. Gasping for air, the creature rakes my face with its razor claws, tearing away flesh down to the bone.

Pain. Absolute pain.

My vision dims. The bogart attacks again and I do anything I can to stop it. Blood spewing from my face, I reach for some-thing, anything I can use to protect myself. My hand slips on the wooden nightstand from all the blood. I use the table as a shield. Scrape after scrape, the bogart chips away at the wood. Any second it will give and there will be nothing I can do.

I scan the floor for something but there is nothing. The table breaks, shattering in two, splintering like the door. There is one piece in each hand now.

Not all is lost.

The bogart lashes out and I stake the cursed thing through its one yellow eye, pushing it through the back of its head. Gore spurts onto the wall and floor.

I push the fiend off me, shaking from the pain radiating from my face. Groping around in the morning light, clenching my face with one hand, I find the Bawaka blade with the other and pull it close, swearing it will never leave my side again.

Staggering to my feet, the situation is dire. Screams continue from outside and I hear glass breaking in the hall. I do my best to ignore the pain, quickly dressing, and strapping my proofing to my sweat-stained skin. My boots slide on with ease and I make a quick check on the wood stakes at my belt.

Plunging into the hall, I find the way is blocked. Bogarts line the corridor in either direction. Their heads turn at the same time, focusing on me. The odds are impossible.

I react instantly, severing a head off the closest one. It collapses to the floor and three more move in to replace it. Scraping, growling, the noise echoes throughout the high ceilings of the hall. They fight to get past one another to get to me. Each wants their chance to kill me. But I see their flaw is numbers. So many of them hinders their movement in the narrow passage, making my work easier. Maybe I can still escape.

Severing another head, I spin around, facing the bogarts approaching behind me. The situation of limited space is the same.

Slash and turn. Slash and turn.

Before long, I am covered with entrails, some stickier than others. I'm not sure how long I can keep this up. I will tire soon. I wonder at the endless supply of bodies. Where are they coming from? Has the whole town turned monstrous?

A bogart breaks through my routine and latches onto my blade with its teeth just missing my wrist. I twist and its face splits like a melon. Sweat drips into my eyes and stings the wound across my face.

Slash. Turn.

The hallway bursts into flames. I flinch from the suddenness of it. Intense heat flares at my back and causes my face to burn. I try to shield it, but it does nothing. The bogarts are on fire. They screech, burning away in twisting swirls of crimson and orange.

The smoke clears and I see Bronin at the end of the hall, no longer dressed in his flowing red and white robes. He is threaded in black shirt and pants, taut to his skin. He tosses a flask of holy water, shattering it on the ceiling above him. As the water rains down, it reacts with the bogarts' skin, burning their flesh. The flames of God.

Bronin mouths something to me, but the noise drowns out everything. His gesture suggests coming to him, so I sprint. Up close, I see he is strong in physique, and agile of foot. The standard robes from before were deceiving; there is no doubt, the man can hold his own.

"What happened?" I shout over the noise.

He pulls a flask from the satchel around his shoulder. "The barrier lamps went out somehow. We need to get out of here." His face is stern, nothing like the night before when he blessed Isabella.

"What about the organ? You can save the church."

"Nester is taking care of that." He pushes me aside, throwing the flask of holy water down the hall. "We are wasting time."

Screams echo through the corridor as we make way for the exit.

We clear the musty interior of the church and are greeted by the gloom of the morning. The courtyard is lost. Scattered fires and rising smoke, survivors fight for their lives. The undead inhabit every inch of the yard, and my hope for escaping dwindles.

Descending the stairs, a man is eviscerated before us. Gnashing teeth rip the flesh from his bones, christening me in blood. Two women, backs to one another, fend for their lives, swinging flaming logs to defend themselves. They are surrounded and before I say anything, Bronin is headed straight for them.

Scanning the courtyard, I search for Kronklich, but he is nowhere to be found. The barrier lamps are certainly out, and for what reason I do not know. Something isn't right. The gate at the wall is demolished, caved in from assault. Impossible. The bogarts have no understanding of organized attack.

Without warning my shoulder explodes with pain and I am sent tumbling down the slippery stairs, landing in a shallow pool of blood. Whose blood it is—I don't know. The metallic liquid drips from my lip and I spit, trying not to vomit. Instinct has me back on my feet, boots sinking in the mud. Hair wet with blood, it stings my eyes as I stare at my attacker.

Steadily descending, a caretaker spastically heads my way with a rusted glowing lamp swaying from its hand. I have to avoid it at all costs, for within the lantern resides its soul. It seeks a new host to harbor a new body to care for. If it goes uncontested, the cycle will repeat, claiming new lives as its own, rotting away to a skeletal frame once again.

No emotion, no sound except for the clicking of its bones on the stone steps. It reaches the muddy ground and continues toward me. I hurl the Bawaka, letting it spin wildly. Impact causes the caretaker to explode, dropping its lantern and releasing the trapped howling soul within. As quickly as the blade left my hand, it returns.

Two bogarts rush me in unison, one latches onto my chest plate with teeth, the other, the bracer on my forearm. I slam them together, cracking their skulls and tossing them aside.

A woman falls into my arms, nearly knocking me over, pleading for help. Her face is scratched and patches of her hair are missing. There are sinewy threads exposed at the neck. "Please my lord, help me." I avoid her eyes while pushing her away and cut off her head with my blade, knowing her fate was sealed.

Where the hell is Kronklich? I look back over my shoulder and see Bronin making quick work of bogarts with his holy fire. The two women he went to save lie dead on the ground, pieces of their faces peeled apart and scattered in the dirt.

I continue searching for Kronklich and find myself frozen to the spot. Nester is running across the courtyard, swinging a studded mace into oncoming caretakers. There is something in his arms that I cannot make out at the moment, but realization strikes me when I hear the cry of a baby. Manson.

I move faster than I ever have, slashing away bogart limbs and scattering caretaker bones. Nester is unaware of the demons behind him. The Bawaka races forward shredding everything in its path, cutting down one, two, three bogarts, before it is suddenly lodged in the breastbone of a caretaker. My legs cannot carry me fast enough to Nester. The bogarts swarm him from every angle. He is doing everything he can to keep the hellish beasts from reaching Manson, forfeiting his own protection. They bite into his arms and legs and back, stripping pieces of muscle and fatty tissue. Instead of crying out in pain, he laments to God. "Holy Father, protect your child!" Blood runs the length of his body as he is brought down. Manson, bundled in blankets, falls from his hands unnoticed, nearly trampled into the blood soaked ground.

My stake impales the first bogart I reach, piercing its neck and immediately I retract it for a second strike to the temple. It splinters, yet I use it again for the next bogart, driving it deep into its chest of purplish skin. I know it won't kill it, but it slows nonetheless. Drawing a second stake, I pierce another bogart through its arm just as it reaches Manson, its infectious claw having groped at the blankets. With both hands I grip the bogart's head and twist, harder than before. There is such malice in my heart. I rip its bony head from its neck ceasing all its possibilities to function. It slumps to the ground in a dripping heap. Breathing heavily, I know I am reaching my limit. But I can't stop now.

Manson is crying frantically as I scoop him up into my arms. His small nose is streaming mucus and tears overflow his eyes. Poor child. He has suffered enough already. His dark, watery eyes stare into mine and for a moment he stops crying. At least one soul will survive this night, I promise myself.

The sudden neighing of horses grabs my attention. Kronklich veers around the back end of the church, three horses drawing the carriage. Brandishing his crossbow, he fires while holding the reigns. His skill is precise, but he is outnumbered. The bogarts are fast behind the buggy. Some cling to the carriage, some to the horses' backs. One bogart tears deeply into one of the horses' necks. The buggy begins to lose its momentum. At this rate, the horses will be eaten.

Cradling Manson in one arm, I run toward the carriage, retrieving my Bawaka from the Caretaker's rib cage. Manson's cry draws the attention of the courtyard as the bogarts react and are quick at my heels. I shout at Bronin to come along but there is no telling if he can hear me. The screams of death drown out everything. I dare not look back.

A bogart's head, directly in front of me, explodes into fragments and I know Kronklich is watching us. Reaching the horses, Kronklich, in a frenzy, leaps from his post, drawing his sword from the cane and slashes. His cover provides enough time to cut the bridle and harness from the dying horse. Without the strain of its attachment, the horse staggers a few feet and collapses. The bogarts swarm, scraping past each other, eager to taste the fresh horsemeat.

It's now or never. "Kronklich! Get us out of here!" I shout over the whinnying of the horse.

With a quick spin and flash of the blade, Kronklich removes two heads and is back on top of the carriage, fending off two more.

Softly, I lay Manson on the floor of the buggy, the safest area I can think to place him. Growling behind me alerts me to a bogart's claw scratching the surface of my proofing before I sever it. The creature retracts from the carriage howling.

"Hyaa! Hyaa!" I hear Kronkilch shouting and the carriage lurches forward with a jolt. The buggy gains speed as I stick my head out the side window. There is no sign of Bronin. The smoke has engulfed all of the courtyard.

Having faith in Kronklich's driving, I retreat back inside. I hover over Manson like a sentinel, guarding him from any foe that might breach the interior. The carriage shudders twice, then it turns hard to the side. For a moment I think it will overturn, but, rocking side to side on two wheels, somehow the carriage straightens and there is another thump.

A pair of hands suddenly grips the window and I breathe a sigh of relief. They are old and human. Bronin is at the window, his blue eyes contrast with the sweat and dirt covering his face. He seems out of breath as he scans the interior of the coach, eyes darting to and fro. "Where is Nester?" he says in a hopeful tone.

I am tired and all I can do is stare at him. I follow his gaze as he looks at the floor where Manson lies. No words describe the look on his face. Losing Nestor for him was like losing a son. I know the feeling.

I help him through the small window as best as I can. We both collapse onto the seat and I can tell he is spent, despite his strong physique. Tears run down his face, and I turn away out of respect.

I look out the window at the fires and smoke pluming into the sky from Albestan Church. The image grows smaller and smaller as the carriage steals into the morning, racing away from the madness and chaos. With no one manning the organ, the church is lost, that is certain. As we pass each street, bogarts and caretakers emerge from alleys and cross streets. Monsters seem to be everywhere, walking freely in the dreary light.

I look over at Bronin. He is turned on his side, arm extended, fingers touching the small hand reaching out from the blankets on the floor. I watch this touching moment of innocence with reverence, knowing that all my efforts have not been in vain. Leaning down, I do the same. I stroke Manson's smooth head, running my fingers along his brow and grazing his cheek. The little man smiles at me, and my body shutters in memory of Dorian when he was a babe, clinging to his mother's breast, smaller than the width of her shoulders.

Thinking my son might be dead, dread fills me.

No. I mustn't think of it. I need to think positively. I will do anything to keep this boy alive. I swear it to myself. I must, if I am to keep my sanity.

CHAPTER
IX

IT IS IMPRACTICAL TO ADMINISTER medicine while moving in a fast-traveling carriage, but there is no choice. Each bump sends searing pain across my face as Bronin treats my wounds. Picking dirt and small pebbles from my torn skin, I feel the wounds are deep. Three succinct slashes just underneath my right eye, the topmost tear having gone deep enough to penetrate my high cheekbone. A dull ache lingers and I realize I need rest.

It is almost midday now and the monsters appear to be congregating toward the town of Roland, as if summoned to a higher calling. We pass them on the road, some of them seeing us, giving chase until we outrun them. Nothing makes sense— except the knowledge we dare not stop.

Manson has been crying for some time now. With the lack of provisions, there is nothing much any of us can do for him. He is only a babe, six to nine months at most. He must eat but I can't risk stopping the carriage to forge for food. The only hope I have is that we reach Cordova Woods soon. There, at least we can find cover to hide the carriage and have a better chance of finding sustenance, some berries or nuts perhaps. I tried mashing hard rationed bread with water earlier, attempting an edible paste to hold him over. But it was to no avail.

"I'm afraid it's going to leave scars," says Bronin digging a swab deeper into one of the cavities on my face.

I can hardly breathe from the pain. "There are far worse things than these scars."

He offers me a hand mirror, but I wave it away.

"I don't blame you for being angry, my son," he says kneeling down and holding the mirror out in front of Manson. The boy stops crying momentarily.

Anger is an understatement. Ever since last night, my entire world has gone to hell. I'm not entirely sure anger sums up any of it. I think about the work I have done in God's name and wonder why the only rewards have been death and more death. No, I'm not angry at God—I hate him.

"Do not hate God," Bronin says suddenly, as if reading my thoughts.

I look at him in wonder, trying to discern if he is in contact with the Holy Father at this very moment, receiving divine council, reading my mind.

"He has a plan for everyone. A divine plan. There are reasons why lives are given . . . and taken. God's will is supreme, Tenor. Have faith."

But Bronin must know that I am bitterly far from faith.

My face stings from the antiseptic and I move over to the window, allowing the cool air to soothe it. I watch the landscape as it passes by, rocks and rolling hills for miles out with the occasional tree jutting from eroded soil. At some point I must have dozed off, for now I am watching large trees pass rapidly before me, overlapping one another as the carriage continues to jostle along The Great Carpella Road. The day has grown darker. Looking up, the canopy is thick with reds, yellows, and browns. Aside from the horrible stiffness in my neck, my face is numb and cold from sitting at the window. At least for a while I won't be reminded of the affliction on my face.

I wonder how Kronklich has been faring all this time, not having given the horses or himself a rest since the attack at the church. As I'm about to climb up to the post to relieve him, I see something passing through the woods just beyond the tree line. A deer perhaps. The mist gathering is shrouding my view. I can't discern quickly enough what it was I saw, but my hopes are raised at the thought of meat for supper.

Now there are more keeping pace alongside the carriage. There is no doubt I see fur. They move, bouncing around the woods, dodging fallen trunks and springing through ferns like all deer do.

My eyes remain transfixed until the ache returns to my face, ending my temporary mercy. Deciding to climb out to relieve Kronklich again, Bronin abruptly grabs my shoulder, giving me a good shake.

"You should stay in the carriage," he says in a concerned tone. I follow his pointing finger and see wolves trailing behind the carriage. Mouths open, their tongues flap in the icy wind, salivating for the opportunity of a meal. They are much larger than normal. I know they are not wolves.

Ducking my head back in, I reach for the case under the seat, unfasten the lid, and make a quick count of our arsenal. Manson is beside me, staring up at me with those dark eyes. His face looks stern for a babe, but at least he is not crying. I reach for a bundle of long silver stakes, and a small quiver of bolts. Double-checking to be certain the Bawaka is secured at my side, I toss Bronin a silver stake and prepare to exit the carriage.

Again, Bronin stops me. "What's this for? They're just wolves."

The look I give him states otherwise. "I'll be right back." As I open the carriage door, it slams back in my face, stinging my nose. Something large is on the other side. Long thick claws rip at the door, breaking through wood, splitting it like fragile sticks. The door is smashed through and a creature, half man and half wolf, waits in its stead. A willderman. It grips the sides of the doorframe and extends its neck, growling with long teeth exposed.

Pulling a silver stake from the bundle, I ram it through the chest, pushing harder and harder to penetrate as deep as I can. The smell of singed hair fills the carriage. The willderman howls, causing my ears to ring; hot blood sprays my neck and face. It clenches the stake with both hands and plummets from the side of the carriage, slamming into a tree with a loud crack.

I duck just in time, dodging a claw aimed for my head. Forced back inside, I see Bronin standing over Manson as I reach for another instrument of death. He holds fast with his stance, but I can tell he's never used a stake before. "If you can, aim for the heart."

Before finishing my words, I duck just as he impales one of the beasts behind me through its face. It twitches at the end of the shaft and the silver reacts with its skin and fur, singing it like mutton over a spit. My boot sends it tumbling from the carriage.

"Thanks," I say to Bronin, realizing I'd been quick to judge.

He nods his head while gripping the stake with white knuckles.

The sound of rushing water draws my attention to the other window of the carriage. Hair whipping about, I survey the steep cliff next to us; water rushes and churns at the far bottom of the ravine. The Faust River. We are getting closer to the ruins of Egleaseon castle.

A loud crack sounds in the distance. A sudden swerving of the coach sends me stumbling backwards, nearly tripping over Manson, then the ground shakes from an explosion. The vibration causes the carriage to rattle and lurch.

Through the new gaping hole in the side of the carriage, I survey the tree side of the road. A massive oak lies sprawled across the path behind us.

"James!" I shout.

It's hard to hear Kronklich's voice over the howling wind. "Everything is under control, Lord Wolfgang."

Under control?

Another sudden turn and I tumble out of the carriage, gripping the exterior side with both hands. My silver stake spins helplessly away, hitting a tree. I can barely hold on as Kronklich continues to explain our situation.

"They're trying to run us from the road," he says pointing to a group of figures in the distance. They seem human, holding axes in their hands, chopping away at a large trunk next to the road. "They're using the trees as blockades," he shouts. "Can you believe it?"

I try to better my situation and nearly slip but something is pulling me.

Looking down, a willderman has trapped my leg against the carriage frame, its claws caught in the buckles of my boot. I try to kick it, but every hit is useless against this tenacious creature. It is impervious to my bludgeoning attempts. It swipes at my leg, trying to peel the proofing off my leg. Its half-man half-wolf snout extends and clamps down, teeth sinking into the leathery surface of my plate armor. The pressure from its jaw is there, but the penetration is stopped. Teeth firmly lodged, I thrash my leg about, dislodging its grip and a few of its canines. Again I kick, and this time it yelps like a wounded dog.

There is a bristling at my back. My neck stings from the branches whipping me as the carriage swerves closer to the tree side. I press my body flat, kicking the willderman square in the jaw. It reaches to bite again and then I feel a large mass scrape the back of my proofing. There is a sickening crunch and the beast is knocked from the carriage. With my foot free, I am able to secure myself and pull myself up the side.

Hoisting my body up, another beast howls in my face. A bolt passes into its brain and it flops to its side, rolling off the roof from the speed of the carriage. Kronklich is sitting at the post, reloading his crossbow with one hand, driving with the other.

I scour the tree line, noticing the beasts regrouping in the midst beyond the trees, keeping pace with the carriage and sprinting far ahead of us.

"Here comes another," warns Kronklich. A massive tree groans as it descends, at first vertically, gaining momentum and then lulling to its side. "Hold on!"

The carriage suddenly careens toward the cliff side. There is a moment where I see the river directly below me. A tingling sensation passes through my hands and feet and a knot swells in my throat. The wheels scrape the edge of the road, dislodging pebbles, spitting up dirt. But the carriage remains true, its free spinning wheel locking in with traction, and the carriage rattles in response.

"Not to worry, Lord Wolfgang," Kronklich says without looking back. Still he formally addresses me.

The carriage jostles as another beast clings to the backside of the carriage. Quickly, I use the dagger from my belt and impale its hand. The creature screams and gnashes its teeth at me, but is completely helpless. Hand pinned, body hanging, it scrambles to gain its footing off the side but instead scratches the body of the carriage. As I reach for the Bawaka at my hip, something stops me. Manson. He is no longer crying, but screaming.

Leaving the willderman to its fate, I drop to my chest, grip the roof of the carriage and drop through the threshold of the gaping hole. I am speechless.

Bronin poises a silver stake before one of the beasts. Gripped by his leg, Manson dangles from its clutches, crying hysterically, as if the beast were examining a piece of meat.

"In God's name, release him, foul beast!" says Bronin, wildly thrusting his weapon.

"No!" I counter, putting my body between Manson and the spear. The silver stake breaks through the front of my right shoulder, just between the proofing and bone.

I shudder.

Pain travels down my arm and up into my neck like poison. There is a sick feeling in my stomach as the willderman rakes its claws at me. I slam my body into its hairy chest, forcing it to drop Manson to the floor. Through Manson's screaming, I hear a loud crack sounding off in the distance. With bare hands I bludgeon the willderman's skull against the side of the carriage over and over, spurting blood and fur all over.

"Take Manson," I manage to say before hearing the neighing of horses and the sound of wood breaking. My head hits the ceiling as everything takes flight. Everyone in the carriage hovers in midair as if gravity had no place. Outside the window, the ground becomes the sky and the sky becomes the ground. The last thing I remember is my body passing through the carriage window into the open air.

CHAPTER
X

INSTANTLY I COME TO. THE shock is sudden and my body strains from the freezing water entering my lungs. My blood turns cold and my limbs go numb, twisting and tumbling like a rag doll through rushing currents, crashing into rocks. It is too cold to feel anything. Panic summons every ounce of energy I have. As I search for the surface, dark water stings my eyes. All I see is decayed life trapped at the bottom of the river. Animals. Humans. All rotted to skeletons. I am running out of air. My chest is about to burst. My arms and legs move me upward but I feel nothing.

I break the surface, air rushing into my lungs. My body bobs up and down like a buoy until it comes to rest between two rocks. Wedged in a crook, the rage of the river assaults me, splashing my face, drowning me without mercy.

Pain returns as blood flows back into my body. Shoulder pierced, face shredded. Both throb with burning cold. My whole body shakes. I can't see the sky, but I know the bleak of twilight is not far off. Thick mist obscures everything above the cliff. The high wall disappears into nothingness. I hear howling in the distance.

Pulling myself onto the rocks, I cough and discharge the rest of the water from my lungs. My head spins from looking around and my vision blurs with hues of red and yellow, distorting anything I see. Souls burn all around me. Has death come for me? No, I've faced it before. This is different somehow. Tentacles reach for me. Hellish claws grope at my skin. What are they?

"Stay away from me!" I shout, choking on more water. I cough and shake my head to rid myself of illusory visions. The wounds on my body burn badly. The water no doubt, mixed with the blood is heightening my pain.

This is the River of Faust, the cursed river that flows uphill instead of down, raging on to the evil at the base of Egleason's ruins. The qualities of the water staunch the blood of my wounds, yet I feel myself going mad. I squeeze the temples of my forehead in desperation and the visions finally fade.

Where's the carriage?

There is a wooden wheel on the opposite bank. My heart sinks. No one could have survived the fall into the ravine, yet here I am, alert and very much alive. The feeling of loss consumes me. Everything I've fought for up to this point came to nothing.

And then, realization sets in. I am utterly alone. Kronklich, Bronin, Manson. My thoughts become darker at the thought of having lost the boy, Manson, left to the willdermen to tear his flesh from his tiny bones. I was his angel, his guardian of hope. But I am no angel.

I wonder if God is above, amused, watching me, watching me fail, seeing what I aim to do next. But it is not He who I sense watching me. Something else is here, some presence I cannot describe. There is a creeping mist moving along the bank of the river, covering the ground like a cloud covers the sky. Within the sinister energy, I see eyes with stalks swaying above mossy mounds of green and brown, clinging to rocks and stones like snails. They are life forms that once served as sentinels for Egleaseon, their purpose now long forgotten. I stare at a patch of eyes close to me and they never blink. They are always watching, so I look away.

I am cold and can't stop shivering. Slowly I stand up from the slick rocks and I nearly tumble back into the black water. I catch myself and stagger. The eye moss follows my every move.

The land along the bank is clear of debris, clear of things that might have been thrown from the carriage. No wood, no weapons, no—bodies. I make a quick inventory of what I have left and find my situation grim. Aside from the proofing strapped to my body, my only other possession is the Bawaka blade strapped to my hip. I thank myself for not using it on the carriage.

I move along the bank, following the flow of the river as my guide. High walls on both sides. I am a trapped animal, vulnerable among the sparse trees and open rock face. Thoughts of my dead companions are all that can comfort my loneliness. Despite the amount of water inhaled, my lips are parched and my throat is dry. I stare at the water rushing by and force myself to look away. What is my preference for ways to die—from madness or from thirst?

Focus Tenor. You need to find Dorian. He is the only thing left on this earth that matters to you.

Limping, I stagger along slanted crags, eyeing the river as if it were some great beast. It goes on forever in either direction. There is no choice. Lingering in this wilderness after dark is certain death. So, I press on, staring at rock after rock. I notice the more steps I take, the easier it becomes to walk. And with the cold having reached my inner core, walking is all I can do to keep from freezing to death.

Bones line the path as it narrows to an almost impossible pass. Scattered about, they are human, having succumbed most likely to a similar fate as mine. One corpse, still wholly together, holds onto its patches of leathery skin; its clothes worm-ridden over time, a dead man never to speak his tale. I wonder at the strangeness of silence all around me. There is neither sounds of birds nor the howl of the wolves anymore. Even the songs of insects are absent. There is only the melody of the river.

My progression comes to a halt as the path runs out. In its place, before me lies a massive landslide of boulders and sharp rocks, the result of the cliff eroded away over time. I dread the thought of having to backtrack the way I came or to forge the river. Moving to the edge of the black water, I stand on a flat rock to gain better perspective. A particularly large mass of eye moss is grouped together near the shore. As I move closer, their eyes focus on me. Ignoring the eyes, it is their mossy roots in which I take interest. They are clumped together and trail to the edge of the river. Cautiously I maneuver myself along the slick rocks and find myself standing before a natural bridge protruding from the swirling water. Pieces of it have been eroded away over time.

Boot over boot, I advance, knowing one wrong move will send me spilling into the drink. Halfway across, I hear low croaking sounds coming from the water. They grow louder and louder with each step I take. Unstrapping the Bawaka from my hip, I study the water with caution. The surface is still and I wonder if I'm hearing things. Then something grazes my leg.

I chance looking down and see nothing. The sudden movement compromises my balance. Something hits me a second time nearly causing me to fall forward. My arms flailing, I see it, a spiny fin disappearing below the water. As I regain balance, numerous white eyes appear in the black churning water. I am acutely aware I need to get off these rocks.

Adrenaline taking over my physical pains, I do all I can to make myself less of a target. There is a splash followed by several more and my nerves tell me to duck. I am sprayed with cold water as hundreds of small fish-like creatures arc over my shoulders through the air. One of them doesn't return to the water. It flops around violently on the rock, struggling to upright itself onto its two hind legs. Peering at me with one eye sideways, it turns to face me, revealing a row of interlocking teeth down the center of its flat face. I view what seems to be a cross between a fish and a frog. Opening its mouth, a worm-like tongue slithers between razor points, licking the rock before it.

Gellies.

Immediately I stand up and charge, kicking the blasted thing back into the river. As I attempt to run, I slip with each step, nearly falling into the black liquid.

The gellies become louder. They are relentless, lobbing their bodies at me from the water, forcing me to move ahead recklessly. I need to get to land. The end of the bridge is in sight. I hop over a crumbled rock, advance a step, then two, and suddenly the final rock I step on gives, causing pebbles and moss to strip away into the water. I bend my knees and leap, pushing my boots off of whatever foundation is left. There is a large splash and I find myself tumbling in dust and dirt.

The gellies are all around me and grunt with excitement. There are too many to count. Their flat faces glisten with moisture and their bellies expand like frogs.

Leveling the Bawaka to the ground, I send it arcing away from my body. The blade carves its way through countless ranks of amphibian creatures. One is pierced, while another is tossed aside. The attack is direct and effective, creating a temporary gap in the mass of chaos. A gellie leaps for my face. With free hands, I catch, stopping it from gouging my face. With the Bawaka returning to me, I immediately toss it away, catching the spinning blade with precision. Instead of throwing it a second time, I use it to swipe low at my boots as I hasten to get away. Gellies split apart by my feet and I run for sanctuary.

The gellies are much slower on land than water and soon there is distance between us. I am out of breath and my legs burn. With only the sound of the river rushing by, I am convinced they have given up pursuit. I slow to a walk, keeping my distance from the edge of the water. Being in the shadow of the ravine with the sun nearly set, the temperature has dropped significantly. Desperation sets in as my body continues to shake uncontrollably.

Movement has become crucial to my immediate survival. The only thing keeping me from losing consciousness is the ache of my muscles and the desire to live. Through the thick mist, a large dark mass grows in size. The need for caution escapes me. I can't stop walking or I will fall over. For what I thought was some new obstacle to overcome, the dark mass soon gives way to a large gaping hole in the side of a hill. The river ascends into darkness through an iron gate, filtering items swept away by the water. Loose debris trapped at its base forms a tumbling collection of garbage. For a moment, I cringe at the thought that my way is barred, but I realize there is a door ahead, halfway ajar. With its hinges rusted, I ponder its open state. A strong breeze blows from somewhere above me, causing the mist to clear from the ground.

That is when I notice the bodies.

Rotten and decomposed, their mouths are open with maggots dripping from the orifices of their once discernable faces. Worms slither from hollow sockets. Roaches clamor over articles of clothing. There are five of them, all bearing weapons except for the ones without limbs. Swords. Maces. They seem to have belonged to some sort of raiding party. Vagabonds, gypsies, hunters. It does not matter their previous charge. They are all equals in death.

I stumble and fall before one of the stinking corpses, one much larger than the rest. Most of the body is still intact; there is still blue-jelly residue in the sockets, spared from the pecking of ravens. A stream of maggots trails from the nostril to the large gaping hole in the side of its neck. Some of its provisions are still intact.

Pushing away a rat, I rummage through a small satchel lying next to the dead body. Despite the gore, my mouth waters at the thought of sustenance. Stale bread? Dried corn? Anything will do. The bag is nearly empty save for a leather skin, a dried pork strip, and some oil soiled torches. Maybe I won't die in this miserable place after all.

Cracked fingers from the cold moisture prevent me from gripping the cork in the leather skin, so I use my teeth. Its supple release from the inside graces my lips with stale water that never tasted so good.

Sitting back on the haunches of my thighs, I savor my brief moment of reprieve, yet the cold doesn't let me linger for long. Unfastening the cloak from the corpse's neck, I discard my own and place my new salvation around my shoulders. It smells of decay, but its warmth I welcome. Suddenly Diana enters my thoughts. My memory of her comforts me in this wicked time. I look around with heavy heart, but the mist offers me nothing. I pull the cloak tighter around me.

There is a necklace hanging from the corpse's neck. Sitting for a moment, I stare at it, shaking my head. Reaching forward, I yank the cross, snapping the leather tie. The sudden force slumps the body forward, stirring more roaches and rancid smells.

Taking deep breaths, I dry heave and stagger away to the riverside, trinket swaying in my trembling fingers. I manage to keep the pork strip down as I hold the silver cross out in front of me, rubbing the dew from it, wondering if the power of God resides somewhere inside its tiny form.

Maybe because I'm beyond exhaustion, or starving to death, my mind wanders. Suddenly, I am standing in the throne room of Lord Egleaseon, years ago, right before the fall of his castle. I had come by personal invitation, obliging his request to bring the one artifact that men killed for, The Hand of God. He wanted nothing more than to be human again, to give up the curse he carried for so long. He would repent and God would be merciful. As Egleaseon took the relic from my hand, I witnessed the mercy God provided. All the years of life granted to Egleaseon fell upon him at once. After two thousand years of being cursed, in that fleeting moment, Egleaseon became human. But quick as the transformation took place, so did his flesh decay. I watched his bones crumble to dust. Did he know or was he tricked? I still can't wrap my head around it.

Such was God's mercy. But was it mercy?

I stare beyond the cross now, focusing on the tendrils of water churning rapidly against the rocks. The water flows like the blood of a man's veins, disappearing into the rusty bars of the gate, disappearing into nothingness, deep in the hole of the cliff. It is death that waits for us in the end. Always has been.

I clench the cross in my fist, as if trying to crush the holiness out of it. Everyone I have ever loved has died. Everyone but one, and the chance he still lives is beyond reason. I am a mad man now, searching for my son. I will save him from that bastard Joachim. I can't wait for God to give me guidance. Temperance has left me.

I let the cross slip from my hand and it falls into the river. I wait a moment, listening for something, but nothing happens. Things are quiet and the silence adds to my feeling of emptiness. I push my damp hair from my face, tucking it behind my ear. Looking up, I want to see stars, so I pretend I see them through the mist that obscures everything.

Night approaches and I can barely see my hand. Remembering the torches in the dead corpse's satchel, I turn to retrieve them before I run out of things to see. The mist filters the light like a black cloth. The thought of fire invigorates me. Groping through fading light, I hear the squeak of scattering rats, and my hand falls around leather just as it becomes pitch black. Placing the bag over my shoulder, I remove one of the torches and begin striking stones together. Three taps and the oil catches. A burst of flame lights up the night and prevents the darkness from swallowing me. The light is blinding; it takes a moment for my eyes to adjust.

And when they do I stand firm, wondering if my eyes are playing tricks on me. The hairs on my arms rise.

I am no longer alone.

CHAPTER
XI

FROM ALL OVER THE SURROUNDING territory, moans from the dead creep into my soul and heart. They give off an unearthly sound, something not of this world, seeping through the land as if squeezed through hell's bowels. The red-orange glow of half torn faces slowly advances toward me. I'm surrounded by demons. I blink. This must be hell.

I recall the water I drank. Was it from the Faust River? Between the glare of torchlight and maggots falling from the lechers, my eyes flutter rapidly. Real or not, the Bawaka blade is in my hand before any of them reach me.

Without thinking, I batter one of the lechers with the torch causing embers to spray about my body in a fiery mist. Light is limited so I think twice about using the torch again.

Stepping back, I spin, severing the head of the lecher. Despite decapitation, it continues advancing without consequence. I duck as a mace passes inches from my face. Rolling across the ground, I slice hard, splitting its abdomen, and its torso falls to the floor. As the body hits the ground, it clamors after me, dragging its upper half with its hands. A glimmer of steel catches my eye. Raising my blade, it stops a sword from splitting my skull. Caught within the angle of my Bawaka, I grip the handle firmly and twist, separating an arm from a shoulder. The ground splatters with maggots from where the arm was once attached and the sword falls with a thud. With its other arm, it latches on and pulls itself to me, snapping its rotten teeth. I try to break its grasp, buts its strength is supernatural. I wrestle it upright, changing stances and losing ground. As each lecher approaches, I batter them with the one holding on to me. Their swords and maces sink deep into my now corpse shield, attacking their own kind without care. The evil in this place is strong.

My body is weak. There's not much more I can do against the relentless attackers. Soon they will have their prize.

I stare into the face of the lecher, watching the insects squirm through its nostrils, snapping its teeth at me like some delectable dish. The rot of its breath is enough to make me choke while teeth fall from its moth-eaten mouth.

With my free arm, I ram the torch into its belly and watch it catch fire. The consumption is instant and intense, burning with an unholy flame. The scars below my eye ache and I stagger back, clutching my face. The lecher burns like an inferno. As it shambles around, the sickening moan returns, like the pain of razors slowly filleting the skin back from sinewy muscle. The fire spreads to all of them like a plague and yet they continue their advance.

I fall to the ground, tripping over something hidden in the mist. Another corpse. My pulse quickens as the body jerks to life, mouth moving, arms twitching. It joins its cohorts in their lament of suffering. It reaches for my leg and I scramble back, avoiding its decayed fingers. Eye moss watches my every move, adding to my anxiety. Shoulder burning, I brace my body to stand and I run, unsure which direction I'm headed, swinging the torch back and forth like a mad man, parting the mist.

Torchlight reflects a glint of metal ahead of me—the iron gate at the mouth of the cave. I dare not stop. The wailing is close and I keep running until I slam into the iron bars with my body. I grasp at the cold metal, struggling to keep myself upright. Out of breath, I navigate the outside of the gate, feeling my way to the opening of the door. Entering, I gasp at the sight of heads on spikes, dozens of them jutting up from the dirt like scarecrows watching over crops. I drop the torch and push on the door but it goes nowhere. I use all of my weight a second time leaning against the rusted hinges to force it shut and again, nothing happens.

Then, something slams into me straight on, forcing me through the door, freeing it of its rusted prison. I stagger a moment and regain balance, charging the door as if I were retaliating against the thing that attacked me. The force knocks the lecher to the ground sparing me a precious few seconds. Tugging on one of the headed spikes, I feel it is heavy, and I use every last ounce of strength to pull it from the ground. I wield it like a heavy war sword, thrusting it down into the dirt where the door overlaps with the gate, locking the barrier in place.

Cold dead hands reach through the bars, grabbing my wrists, slamming my face into the cold iron. The rusted edges cut my skin, speckling the metal with my blood. The lecher wails, trying to bite my face, but the bars keep it at bay. Its tongue laps at the fresh blood.

My energy spent, too weak to break free, I'm trapped in a stalemate, this dead thing and I. Through its hollow eyes and empty head, I see the others approaching like demons released from hell to seek out new stock. I cry out as the lecher squeezes my wrists harder, desperate for more than just a taste of blood. It will snap my bones if I don't break free. I can't fail now. "Dorian!" I scream with pain as if his name would release me from my bonds. "Dorian! Dorian!" I can't open my eyes. The pain won't allow me.

The pain increases, moving from my wrists to my face. Blinking tears away, an inferno rages before me as the lecher releases me. They are all on fire now.

I crawl backwards through the dirt, taking deep breaths, wiping grime from my eyes. The taste of metal is strong in my mouth as I stare into the orange and red light. Hell's demons snap their burning faces at me from a distance. They step on one another, grabbing, shoving, trying to get to me. I am a piece of meat dangling in front of their faces. A prize beyond the gate.

But as the moments pass, they burn to black, crumbling to dust one at a time. The charred remains of the damned. All I can do is stare at the emptiness. Weariness overcomes me. The flames from the bodies dissipate. Embers twirl through the gate's bars like fairies dancing through the woods. My head is propped against an iron spike for comfort. Looking up, a skull looks down at me, mouth open, pierced through the top of its head.

I'm so tired. Is it laughing at me? I almost laugh at it.

The moaning and wailing have stopped. Sitting up, the torch still burns. Taking it in hand, I hold it away from my face despite how numb my body is. "I'm in hell," I say to the shadows around me, but there is no response. There is no comfort in this place. I have no choice but to move forward. Going back is not an option, especially if what awaits me is more lechers.

The sound of the raging river is very near and serves as my guide. Cautiously, I move among the spiked heads, varying in decomposed states. Some very old. Some relatively fresh. I smirk at the simple yet barbaric tactic to dissuade those who would trespass the waterway. I feel lightheaded at the thought of Joachim removing the heads of helpless victims. Would Dorian be added to his collection? I have a feeling my answer lies ahead, waiting for me in the dark.

Pebbles tumble under my feet as I near the water's edge. The current looks strong. I watch it run its course through the heart of the underground ruins. The further I travel, the more agitated the water becomes. Mist sprays in the torchlight and cools my face. The sound of the rushing river is calming and is soon interrupted with the creaking of wood. I shake the ridiculous thought of a windmill existing underground from my mind and soon confirm my assumption. Within the minimal light, I make out the beginnings of a wooden wheel spinning. Cupped paddles disappear out of sight, deep under the dark water. It's a mechanism of some sort, an oversized wheel spinning ominously alone. A faint squeak escapes the bearing at its center; rust having tainted its exterior. Realization sets in that I am in the aqueducts of the castle, where water is transferred throughout the grounds and the great wheel turning before me generates power. Such architecture and ingenuity is found in the great cities. I've heard rumors of advancements like this in Egleaseon's castle, but never believed it.

Continuing on, I come across a similar structure but the wheel is frayed and snapped. Large stalactites have fallen through it, splintering it like a storm-blown shack. Support beams, full of rot hold long wooden structures in the air. Flumes. They rise from the river like bent fingers, transferring the rushing water to stone ducts, which in turn feed the bowels of the castle. The sight is bizarre yet I am amazed at the design. There is an abundance of wooden wheels here, some smashed to oblivion, some still in working order, creaking away at the bearings.

More of the castle has fallen in on itself. Structures once complicated in design now lie demolished beyond recognition. Stone and wood are stacked on each other, some obstructing the river, some spread across the rubble. My progression ends as the river suddenly plummets into depths unknown, a waterfall launching off the cliff like an arrow leaving its bow. I cannot imagine what waits at the bottom, and as I stand pondering, I realize there is nowhere left for me to venture.

I turn around and wave my torch overhead. Maybe there was something I missed. An opening, a crack in the wall. Nothing. My search goes in vain and I am left standing before one of the spinning wheels, watching the wet paddles glisten. Affirmation grips me.

Double-checking my possessions, I am assured they are firm to my body. Keeping a tight grip on my torch, I time the rotation of the wheel, hold my breath—and leap.

My body wedges between two paddles. The water is cold and the wood is slick. Ascending with the rotation of the wheel, within moments I am standing erect, waiting for my opportunity.

Just as I thought, I am higher than one of the flumes and jump down with ease. Boots splash into the rounded shape of the interior; the footing is awkward and the entire support system shudders from my sudden weight. There is a deep, drawn-out groan as the flume sways. My heart beats fast and I assure myself this will work and proceed to crouch, arms extending. I focus ahead of me and not below. I advance some and reach a bend. Each step sends beads of water trailing upward instead of down. Holding out my hand, the water trickles between my fingers, constantly moving upward, passing from my hand and into darkness.

The more steps I take, the more creaking there is. I pause, hearing the chirping of the paddle wheels below. Or is the sound coming from above? It is difficult to discern as I tread the water in sodden boots. I'm not sure how high I am and wave my torch above my head. There is a glimpse of grey stone in the distance. My steps quicken at the thought of being closer to the top than I thought.

A loud crack resonates all around me and I am thrown off balance. Suddenly I am weightless and reach for anything I can grab. My hands find purchase at the edge of splintering wood and I grimace. Hanging and swaying in midair, I dare not let my torch go. Without sight, I'm as good as dead.

The squealing wheels get louder as I try pulling my body up onto the flume. The air current picks up.

Something passes my body.

Flapping wings surround me, beating me, unyielding, nearly distracting me from the little grip I have.

Cursed bats! Completely vulnerable and shoulder aching, I groan, heaving my mortal body onto the flume. I drape my cloak over my face and shoulders, covering my exposed flesh and wait for the beasts to finish their frenzy.

The echoes fade away and I continue with caution. The wood groans from my weight again but I have reached the opening in the side of a great stonewall. Water rushes through flawlessly.

Pulling myself through the opening, I am thankful to be standing on stable ground, despite the constant trek through water. Each stone in the aqueduct is mortared with thick roots, brown in color, slick with moisture. Some of them I use to pull myself along the incline, preventing myself from slipping. I pay no mind to the eye moss sighing around me for I am no stranger to them. They shudder from my torch as I pass, cowering from the heat.

CHAPTER
XII

WALKING SEEMS AN ETERNITY. SUPPLIED by the Faust River, the aqueduct seems to go on forever, and my legs begin trembling, but I stop every so often to allow the burn to dissipate. Being in the ruins of Egleaseon's castle, I know any moment something could emerge from the darkness with the want to consume my soul. I smash some of the eye stalks in frustration.

I walk for what seems forever and finally reach the inside of a large rounded chamber. A mass of roots hang from the ceiling like an elegant chandelier in an earthly ballroom. Skeletal figures hang suspended in air like prey caught in a spider's web.

Every direction is the beginning of a new passageway, some accessible, some demolished. Water passes easily through the open ones while the ones laid with rubble collect vertical pools of water like oblong vanity mirrors. My reflection stares back at me as I stand before one. It is the first time I have seen myself since yesterday morning and I am disheveled. The scars beneath my eye are puffy and my hair is greasy, slicked back with wetness. The discoloration in my face is a mixture of blood and dirt and my hands, shriveled like prunes, glow a pasty white. I wonder at the evil energy of this place, sucking the life from me in its own twisted way, feeding off of me, surviving.

Such is the evil of this place. The root of it never died after the castle fell. What would Diana say if she saw me in my present state like this, at the bottom of a dark evil castle, all disheveled and hair a mess. If only I had told her the extent of my work, all the creatures I've slain, the evil places I've been, maybe she'd still be alive. She might have been better prepared for what happened. She and Dorian could be somewhere far away, safe. But the image continues to haunt me, my hands pushing the wood through her heart.

What sounds like voices howling off in the distance returns me to my present state.

Holding my torch before me, the light grey color of the stones allow me to see further than usual. I follow the sound, burning cobwebs away in the process. I'm not sure how many passageways I traverse, but I know finding my way back is futile. Only the sound serves as my guide and for what reason, I do not know.

The tunnel eventually levels out and my legs are grateful for it. With less water racing up the center, my boots have a chance to dry. They click along dry stone, footfall after footfall. After some time, I no longer hear my guide. The howling has abandoned me.

Someone or something has taken its place, watching me from the distance like some anomaly. I move from the center of the tunnel, pressing my body firm against the wall. Yellowish eyes glow in the distance unlike the eye moss I've seen. The glowing orbs move closer and so I move back, arms reaching in the dark, searching for something, anything.

A set of iron rungs protrudes from the aqueduct wall and with haste I begin climbing. Every few steps I look down, checking below, but find nothing. I blink back the dust in my eye and wonder at the wavering glow high above me. Hand over hand, I pull myself along, tired and hungry, trying not to think of sleep. Outlined in the flickering light, I make out some sort of grate, small and circular in nature.

I stop, inches away and look through the small openings. Torches set in iron sconces line the length of a barren wall. Stones similar to the ones in the aqueduct make up the majority of its construction yet they do not glisten with moisture. Surely Joachim must have been this way. Who else would need light to see? I imagine him dragging my son by the arms, unconscious, helpless, to some remote location of these ruins to do God knows what. My thoughts get the better of me and I begin breathing fast. Get a hold of yourself, Wolfgang. Now is not the time to lose it.

Snuffing my torch, I tuck it into my belt, and as I place both hands on the grate, I retract them instantly.

A dark figure passes over, panting, tapping its way along the stone floor. More pass as I wait, taking shallow breaths to limit my sound. A snout appears and sniffs the air. Wet slime drips from its nostrils onto my shoulder. The figure passes back and forth, scratching at the metal. Whimpering and growling, it suddenly stops in response to howling down the hall. The beast has been summoned. It howls after its pack, leaving me unattended.

They are daver hounds. Sick demented animals left to wander the dilapidated halls of Egleaseon's castle. Half wolf and half dog, they once served as the cleaners to the dungeons, smelling the air for the blood and decay of victims. Eating up the rotten remains of prisoners left for dead. I remember them well from years ago when the count's daughter set them on me, doing everything she could to prevent the union of her father and I, when I was welcomed here once and she betrayed that pact of honor. In the end, her attempts to kill me sealed her own fate, bringing my blade across her white neck, severing her immortal life forever. The walls were painted red that day and the daver hounds ate what was left of her body.

Hands back on the cold iron, I take a deep breath and twist. The seals give and I cast the circular disc to the side. Pulling myself through the opening, I am left standing in a long narrow hall, dust ridden and full of cobwebs. Either direction seems an eternity, so I listen to my gut, following after the sounds of the hounds. The hall widens and becomes filled with decorations.

Stepping over piles of bones, ducking under chains, I dare not chance my discovery to some ill-fated maneuver. Every step is crucial as I move through this decrepit place of torture. I pass instruments unknown to me, things conjured from the depths of hell. A throne made of spikes. A rack with turning wheels. A coffin with razors lacing the interior. I notice bloodstains soaked through the petrified wood. Drapes of silk spun sacs cover benches. Spiders crawl from black holes and I am well reminded of Cordova Woods' inhabitants. Cages hang from the dungeon's corners, imprisoning skeletons over the floating dust. Teeth locked in eternal grins, their countenance brings false joy and I imagine them whispering their unforgivable deeds to those who would listen.

Their heads seem to move with me as I pass, but I know they are long dead. Between the light dancing on the walls and the darkness consuming everything, it's a trick of the mind.

Moving beyond this terrible place, the surroundings do not improve. Traversing corridors made of iron bars, these are the holding cells of the dungeon, riddled with flakes of rust and chipped paint. Braced upon a cell door, a skeleton remains propped upright by a set of prison keys in its bony hands. Its hands grip the key rings as if it would die if it let go. There is rope tied around the wrists and I wonder why it would attempt to reenter a cell that it was no longer in.

The howl of the daver hounds causes the hair on my arms to rise. I see their shadows moving along the far corridor in the distance. I cannot run anymore and they will be on me in moments.

As I grab the keys from the skeleton's hands, its body crumples, scattering bones across the floor. Prying its hands off, I cast them aside and attempt to turn the key in the hole. It doesn't work. I try again, shaking the contraption violently and suddenly there is a click. With a groan the door barely opens and I wedge myself through. My satchel snags on a protruding hinge and I struggle with it. It won't budge and I'm forced to leave it hanging on the frame. Door clanging shut, key turned in the lock, the hall is flooded with daver hounds. For a second time this night a gate has saved my life.

Scrambling into the darkness of the cell, I watch the dogs tear into my satchel, ripping the bag from the strap, shredding it like a helpless animal. The beasts fight over its contents of dried pig skin. My water skitters across the floor, kicked away along with the torches. Watching the grey-skinned monsters finish off the last of my food, my stomach growls in response despite how sick I feel. Some of them look around sniffing the air, unsatisfied, hoping to find another meal and that's when I notice the veins that run shallow below the surface of their skin. Purple and red, they protrude superficially, oozing blood from their backs, dripping onto the floor. One howls, then the rest follow. The pigskin is all gone and suddenly I realize that was what they were after.

Slumped against the back wall, tucked away in the shadow, I welcome the comfort of the cold cell, for I am tired beyond thought. My eyes flutter and I struggle to keep them open. Images of the hounds pass my vision, running up and down the hall in a frenzy. Sniffing the air again, they seem to have found something new.

Darkness comes quickly. Listening to the howls of the daver hounds echo through the halls lulls me to sleep.

CHAPTER
XIII

LIGHTNING PIERCES THE NIGHT SKY, bathing my surroundings in quick blazes of sheer white. Thunder rattles my bones as my finger-nails sink deep between the pieces of bark soaked with rain. With my strong grip, my balance is secure high up in the tree. The branches sway in the storm and the leaves block the view of my destination. My hair pulled tight in a high knot does nothing to stop the water from dripping down the tip of my nose. I blow the excess liquid from my lips, tasting its suppleness from the trees.

All around me the storm rages and I am confident my presence will go unnoticed. The two-story structure beyond the canopy of redlings reveals large trees with rusted leaves that flash alive with each lightning strike. Their metallic hue shimmers in the rain.

Muscles tense, I step away from the tree's base and run the course of a thick branch, using the knots of broken limbs to secure my footing. Moving like a greydan leopard, I descend quickly, catching branches to swing myself from one onto another. The process is re-

petitive and easy, and the last branch I touch breaks. I land on the balcony of a wooden porch without a sound; the rain ravages around me. Everything is as should be. The clap of thunder. The gust of wind. Silence stirring within noise.

Shielding my eyes from rain, I see the large expanse of window before me, separated by one beam of wood through its center. There is little light to see with, but the frequency of flashes is enough to show my reflection in the glass. My face is smooth and chiseled, young and flawless, my blue eyes dark from the shadows of the blacksmith's home. Old man Dora. He would murder me if he knew I was here.

Crouched like a feral cat, my reflection creeps up to the glass and that's when I notice the warm glow of candlelight from within. Wet hands on the glass, I slide the window carefully, not making a sound despite the wood catching the warped frame. My face is caressed with warmth and sweet fragrances. My pulse rises as I step down onto a wooden chair, knowing I am in dangerous territory. It creaks from my weight, but the sound of rain outside the open window is louder.

Closing the window seals the room off like a vacuum, dulling the outside noise in an instant. My boots dripping from the rain, I creep quietly past a vanity and there is a flash of lightning, brighter than the few candles along the bedside tables. The candle flames waiver slightly from a draft under the closed door across the room. A pottery wheel sits in the corner, glistening with wetness. Buckets sit by the legs, full of thick grey substance—clay I'm almost sure. A collection of vases line the far wall along with canvas paintings of red and white peony flowers. I realize I've stopped to admire the work and curse myself. A noise comes from the bed.

Bending at the knees, I move over to the door and check the handle. Locked. With my plan well in order, I move to the foot of the bed and stare at that which I have come for. My prize. My abysmal ocean.

She is nestled in blankets of mauve and peach. The quilt has been cast aside, revealing her tender body. She is turned on her side and I watch her breasts rise and fall, ribs expanding and shrinking. I imagine my fingers tracing the grooves of her delicate bones, caressing each path, a journey into ecstasy. Her navel, white as snow, escapes the blankets ever so slightly, and I know delight waits for me.

Carefully I slip each boot off, placing them next to the brown chest, followed by my sodden clothes. The warmth of the room fills my naked body as I climb onto the bed, distributing my weight as best I can. Thunder rattles the wood ceiling and floors, and my beauty stirs in the nest of softness. A sigh escapes her lips, but it's not of discontent. The storm outside has triggered some thought in her dream world, for her eyes flutter, but she does not wake.

I am above her, staring at her peaceful sleep, yearning to wake her, to show her that I've come, but my waiting is no longer needed. Her dark eyes open, and instantly I am lost in her darkness.

"Curse you, Tenor," she whispers as her slender fingers grip the side of my torso. "Father will kill you if he finds you here." Her touch is warm as she pulls me close to her, spreading her body before me, inviting all aspects of my being to join her in dreamland.

I am burning.

Immediately my tongue samples her flesh, running the crevice between her soft breasts and stops at the first rib, the ribs I so desperately longed for. I nibble some and move onto the next, and then the next until I've run out of ribs to kiss. I press both of my hands down on her hips, forcing her into the plush of feathers. She moans softly and I know she is ready. Moving my face to meet hers, I kiss her lips and she bites mine. I bite her neck and she kisses mine. Her face turns and I kiss her cheek and suddenly her hand touches my stomach and I shudder. She gropes further down, traveling well beyond my pelvis, helping herself to the pleasure ready for her. She guides me. Inside, I feel myself connect. My lust grows with each thrust. I love this woman. Her hands run the course of my arms moist from the rain. A moan escapes her lips again, louder than before.

"Shhh," I whisper in her ear and I cover her mouth. "Your father will hear."

Her response is thrusting me deeper into her with her hands on my back. Pure bliss is what I feel. "I love you, Diana," I say. She smells so good. There is a sweetness about her that ignites the fire within me. It won't be long now.

"Don't," she tells me. "Not yet," she begs, but I am lost in her eyes and I cannot do what she asks of me.

Afterwards, we lie side by side, covered in sweat. The room is warmer than before and I'm not sure how much time has passed. Her arm rests on me, tracing circles on my chest. I sense she trusts me. That I will be there for her always to protect her from harm. I kiss her fingers.

I turn my head, and she does the same and I become lost in her sea of blackness once again. "I will tell him tomorrow," I say in a low voice. She looks at me as if I were mad. "The hunter will have the blacksmith's daughter. It must be so."

"What of your family, Tenor?" she asks. "The boundaries you'll cross."

"The bond has never been broken in my family. They will support me. They'll understand." There is worry in her eyes. They glisten with tears and I wipe away a streaming trail. "If anything were to happen, we would start our own family." I clutch her hand in mine, making a fist, and placing it over my heart. "Our son will be a greater hunter than me."

Each of my wrists is bound with a leather bracelet, heirlooms to the house of Wolfgang. Unbuckling one, I wrap it around her wrist, ensuring its perfect fit. I kiss her hand and she climbs on top of me.

"No one is a better hunter than you," she says. Her body is so light and slender.

A sharp rap on the door interrupts my train of thought and suddenly my head hurts.

"Diana," comes a muffled voice from the other side of the door. It's old man Dora.

"Father!" she whispers. "It's my father! You must leave! Now! Or he will kill you." The terror in her eyes dilates them like twin abysses. She shakes me hard, but I don't want to leave. I never want to leave her side. "Tenor! My father! He's going to kill you!"

DAY THREE

CHAPTER
XIV

THE PAIN IN MY HEAD is excruciating, as if knives were poking and dissecting the fascia of my brain. Memory has eluded me. There is a voice somewhere and my body suddenly moves. I'm not the one moving it. I want to ignore it, but I'm manipulated, molested. My Diana, my beauty. She is gone. I will kill the person who took her from me.

"Wolfgang. Lord Wolfgang!"

Whispers echo about me but I can't open my eyes. My body moves again and this time I feel a hand on me.

The demons are back. They will not take me. I'll make sure of it.

I grip the arm of my assailant, disregarding the fire that will burn me, and my eyes flick open. Wrinkled face. Crystal blue eyes. Someone is staring at me and his grip is strong.

"Wake up, my son. Wake up!"

The man shakes me violently. There is a brilliant fire next to his face. A torch burning hot. Scratches and splotches of blood cover his face.

"Blessed be to God, I thought you were dead," he says, gripping my face, looking me over like a manic parent.

I thought the same.

Everything is blurry. My wrist hurts where the lecher placed its hand on me yet I rub the other one, the one that no longer carries the bracelet of my family. My blessed Diana. What is she doing to me? A chill races up my spine at the thought of touching her again.

Father Bronin's hand is before me and I push it away, still unsure if what I'm seeing is real or not. It's hard to discern what he's thinking, hard to ignore the expression on his face. His tight black clothes are torn and full of dust and grime. He is trembling some, but not as much as I am. I shiver despite the blazing torch.

"Lord Wolfgang. It's me, Father Bronin. God knows what you've been through." He shakes his head while smiling, "His will saved you from that fall."

I recall falling from the cliff and suddenly flinch, remembering the impact into the icy water. The freezing cold. The sharp needles through my body. The memory is forever imbedded.

"I thought you were dead when the carriage flipped, but I was wrong. How very wrong I was." He pauses. "Forgive me. I lost hope."

I feel joy at his words that he concerns himself for me. Such enthusiasm. I'm tickled really. But something bothers me, and it's not the throbbing headache at the front of my skull. I look around the dank cell, vision spinning some, remembering its walls of mortared roots, cracked grey stones and cobwebs. A faint recollection of howling seeps from my thoughts and quickly I move against the bars, pressing my face in either direction to see if the daver hounds were gone.

"Where are they?" I stammer out, swallowing against the dryness of my throat.

"Tenor?"

"Where are they? Dammit! Where are they!" They will be back. They would have smelled Bronin by now.

"Where is what? No one is here," Bronin says in a soft tone. His face is stoic.

I sink down from the bars, letting my hands scrape along its rusted edges. My hands are cracked and bleeding but I disregard any pain from them. It's the sharp ache in my head that reminds me of here and now. "The hounds," I whisper, more to myself than anyone. "The daver hounds. They were here—rancid skin—dripping veins."

I stop in mid-sentence noticing a satchel lying on the floor of the prison hallway. There is a leather skin lying in the corner, unused torches with flint, and a small package bound by twine. In seconds I have the cloth unfolded in trembling fingers and the familiar scent of pig makes my mouth water. I am hungry beyond measure.

A hand on my shoulder makes me jump and I spin around with blade in hand.

"Are you all right, my son?"

Bronin's eyes bring ease to my nerves as I relax momentarily. I am like a tightly wound spring, ready to snap. Bronin is talking to me, trying to calm me down, talking reason, but my body is beyond reason. The only thing I'm reacting to is pain. Pain is my fuel.

"The evil of this place has plagued you, Lord Wolfgang. You are not yourself," he says reaching for the cross around his neck to give me a blessing. I stare at it. Doesn't Bronin know by now that won't work?

Plagued by evil, indeed. I have known evil my whole life. It has been at my doorstep since I was a child. I wonder what new evil now resides in my life. God himself perhaps? Watching Bronin hold the cross, I wonder. Is this how God sends salvation? Sparing the life of an old man over that of an infant?

"Don't worry about me," I say, watching him stare at the gashes on my face. "I'm fine. What of the others? Kronklich? Manson? Are they dead?" My words are cold and harsh for they have been dead in my mind for some time. Manson's screaming face flashes before me. His tiny chest ripped open by willdermen. And Kronklich. He would never be taken prisoner. I grip my face, squeezing at the temples. God, my head hurts.

"I couldn't find their bodies. I searched the wreckage—I did all I could," says Bronin. The look on his face holds sorrow. The same look he spared me at Albestan Church, when I told him of Dorian's abduction. Bronin continues, "If they have passed, then they are better off than we are, next to our humble God."

Despite my inability to reason at the moment, my mind lingers on the integral circumstance of Bronin, his finding me here, far below the earth, deep within the dark depths of this decrepit dungeon. The cesspool of the castle.

"How did you find me?" I ask him.

Bronin's icy stare wanders over my face again. Sweat drips from his forehead despite the cold air. The torch is brighter than usual and burns ferociously near his head.

"Through God's miraculous powers," he says, waving his hand above his head for effect. "He guided me to you somehow."

I blankly stare beyond him, wanting to confess my true thoughts about God, that he is ruthless and cold, and cares not for the good of man. But I wait. This is not the time or place.

"After the carriage crashed, I was thrown to the roadside, tumbling through the brush," continued Bronin. "I searched the area for them until I could no longer see. The night came fast, faster than I ever recall. So I took refuge here, within these cursed walls, where Dorian might be. I've been looking for him ever since."

The look on Bronin's face is genuine. In his mind I was dead, yet he was here looking for my son. I have no words to express my gratitude. God has done good with his soul. I cannot say the same for mine. Bronin's sudden appearance saved my life. He has food. Water. The fresh liquid never tasted better as it floods my throat. The bread he salvaged from the wreckage is soft in my hands. Its complexion is light next to my filthy skin. He is carrying vials of holy water along his chest strap and a silver stake tucked in his belt. Following my gaze, he holds the stake out to me. "It will serve you better than it did me," he says, glancing at my shoulder. It aches as bad as my head.

Anxiety beseeches me as I look about the corridor. Residual thoughts on the daver hounds haunt me still. They seemed real enough. This place is poison to me. The longer I stay, the more my mind decays. I stand and stretch.

My body is stiff as I move through the hall. The few hours of sleep, if one could call it sleep, seemed to rejuvenate me some. I feel life coming back to me, energy returning to my cramped muscles.

"We should go the other way," says Bronin, pausing in his step, holding his torch out in the direction I came from.

"No," I say firmly. "We must go this way if we have any hope of finding my son." Already I'm thinking of the things I will do to Joachim when I find him.

Bronin runs a hand through his white powdery hair. "I just came from that direction." There is a look in his eyes that speaks uncertainty, almost fear.

"And what did you see?" I ask. "How much of the castle still stands?"

"Hardly any of it. The castle is in ruins, fallen in on itself. I was fortunate to find a path beyond the foyer."

I have no time for this. I continue moving down the corridor. This place might be affecting Bronin's judgment. He doesn't know the things I've seen by the Faust River. The horrors that wait there.

The cells lining the walls are like an endless cage of despair, cellblocks, one after another. Eventually, they end, changing direction. I know Bronin is behind me, his boots are loud along the stones. More turns through the dungeon and finally we reach a set of iron-bound, wooden-planked doors. They are open and riddled with cobwebs. I try not to disturb anything as I progress, knowing that some beast may leap out from the shadows. Skeletons, shackled to the walls like beasts line most of the way from this point on. They remind me of the caretakers that came out of the woods to attack the village. Yet they carry no lantern or soul. They were prisoners left to die from starvation, or worse, to be drained of their blood. The daver hounds have picked them clean.

Corner after corner, we are greeted with our own shadows from the torches. Why would Joachim come this way with Dorian? I'm amazed at the length of the dungeon until at last, we arrive at the foot of a long flight of stone steps.

"This is the way you came from?" I call behind me.

"Yes," Bronin replies, not far behind. His sneezing echoes through the hall. "The stairs ascend around a bend and open into a chamber."

Slowly I begin ascending, still working the blood through my legs. More skeletons with wrists bound behind their backs decorate the base of the walls.

Spiders dangle from loose threads as I swipe my torch side to side, ensuring none of them touch me. The stairs are ancient, cracking from the weight of each step. When we reach the top, I feel it is cramped, the air, flat and stale. I feel claustrophobic at the moment and wish desperately for a breeze of fresh air. But it never comes. Everything smells of mold. The cracks in the walls drip with water. Again my mind ponders Joachim's intent. Why here of all places? This place is a ruin, nothing more than potential for a museum as far as I am concerned. Despite my inclinations, I realize my thoughts are pointless. Yet the further I go, the more anger torments me. I will allow Joachim to confess his sin to me before I rip his throat out. Let him clutch at me while he bleeds all over.

Suddenly, I stop and Bronin nearly walks into me.

"Sorry, didn't know you needed to rest."

But rest is not the reason I've stopped. I see a solid wall before me, and my thoughts turn to doubt. Placing my hands on it, it is cold, and the material is different from the rooted mortar that sets the stones in the dungeon.

I look to Bronin for answers but his eyes are wide. "That wall was never there before."

CHAPTER XV

"Are you certain?"

"Very."

Bronin steps back from the wall as if he'd seen a ghost.

I grab him by the shoulders and shake him. "Are you absolutely sure?"

Bronin's eyes never leave the wall. "I would not have found you if I didn't come this way." He pauses and looks at me. "There is no other way through the ruins."

I have heard the rumors before, the extent of Egleaseon's power over his castle, how he could change its structure at will, its very foundation to his liking. But such a feat now would be impossible. Egleaseon was dead. I witnessed his death first hand. Bronin did as well, as we rode away in the carriage, the castle crumbling behind us.

The evil residing in this place must be lingering. I've witnessed it first hand, the Faust River running in a reverse direction, the aqueduct water falling up instead of down. It's as if this cursed place lives beyond the control of its former master. How could a place live? I want to make sense of it, but the longer we stay, the grimmer our situation becomes. We need to find Dorian and get the hell out of here.

Tapping on Bronin's shoulder, I begin descending the stairs. "We have to go back," I say, cursing at the thought of starting all over. It will be difficult working our way down the aqueducts.

"What do you mean go back?" asks Bronin, trailing close behind.

"We have to go back through the tunnels. There must be a passage I overlooked."

I can't help to think the skeletons we pass seem to say, "I told you so," as we quicken our pace. Our boots carelessly click on each step as we descend. Down and down we go. It seems a never-ending descent. My pace slows. Something isn't right. The stairs should have ended by now.

"What is it?" asks Bronin, standing next to me, staring into the same endless darkness.

"The way we just came. It's gone." I take a few more steps forward and look back. Bronin is still there. "Stay close to me."

Bronin puts his hand on my shoulder and I continue. Despite the numerous torches lit along the stairs, the further I descend, the darker the surroundings. The light fades unnaturally. Another trick? A loud boom suddenly shakes the walls of the passage. A heavy thud, like that of a large trunk slammed shut. I pause to listen, and in the eerie silence, Bronin's breath is heavy. Although he's advanced in his years, he is strong, but I can tell he is not used to stairs.

A new sound echoes up the stairwell, the rattling of many chains.

Bronin taps me on the shoulder and points. "Look."

Something is moving up the stairs. White ashen figures floating in the dark. No skin. No eyes. They glow like apparitions, getting closer and closer still. But they are not ghosts and they are not floating. Skeletal legs emerge from the darkness, dragging black chains, shackled to their feet. Arms hang loosely at their sides. Some are missing their arms and some use the walls to hold themselves up. They are carrying lanterns. I take a few steps back, forcing Bronin to stay behind me. There are so many of them.

I gaze back and it is the same behind us. Dozens of caretakers coming toward us. Their feet scrape along each stumbling step, falling, but not one lantern is broken. Those are intended for the living, souls seeking a new life, a way out of their dying existence. They recover just enough to keep moving.

"Back," I say, never taking my eyes off them. I feel Bronin moving until he stops. Our backs are against the wall with nowhere to go. I hold the torch away from my body, keeping the caretakers at bay. One comes into my circle and I swing, striking its rib cage. Bones scatter across the ground as its lantern falls and shatters. The soul has nowhere to go and dissipates with a howl.

To my left, I hear more glass breaking and see a burst of flame. Some of the skeletons are on fire. They take a few steps closer and crumple to the stairs, falling apart like dolls, bones rolling along the steps. More howls.

"Save your holy fire, Bronin. We need to conserve." But as I say the words, there is no end to the caretaker's approach. Beyond the ones I see, there are more. And beyond them, even more. The corridor, once lost in darkness now emanates an endless supply of lantern light.

A caretaker's head soars through the air as I strike another, but the body still advances.

"What do you suggest I use, my hands?" asks Bronin. Before I reply, he removes one of the torches from the wall and smashes a skeleton through its torso, forcing it to drop its lantern.

I swing with ferocity, hitting skeleton after skeleton, but the effort is futile. The skeletons are swarming us and I'm running out of room to swing. My hand goes to the Bawaka. I don't want to chance losing it, but I have no choice. I raise the blade to throw and suddenly hands clasp my shoulders and I'm thrown back, losing my balance. I fall to the floor and roll to my side just in time to see the wall move back into place, cutting the caretakers off from us.

Bronin is standing next to the threshold, his hand on a torch sconce; then he releases it. A mechanical sound echoes inside the wall. Silence falls over us.

"That was close," he says, adjusting the strap across his chest and picking up the torch he discarded.

Too close, I think to myself.

Thumping and scratching comes from the other side, but the caretakers are sealed off. "How did you know?" I ask.

"What, about the switch?" He moves back to the wall, holding the torch before it as if keeping the caretakers at bay. "I didn't. It was simply—"

"God's will. Yes, I know." Somehow I find that hard to believe.

Looking around, I notice we are in some secret part of the castle. A long corridor runs further than my eyes can see. It is straight and riddled with cobwebs. Wooden rafters support the ceiling. Some distance away, there is a broken one, splintered like a fallen tree. The area is cramped and tight, so I stoop, making sure my head doesn't hit anything. The passage glows eerily from long tapered candles, flickering as I pass. Walking for some time, I get the sense the passage is similar to the stairs we encountered. That it might go on forever or change. I look back and Bronin is some distance from me, steadily following. I am thankful for his company, but my desire to be alone surfaces again when I recall my moment with Diana. I wonder if it's this passageway that summons my thoughts. I'm not sure, but I cannot quell the urge at the moment. It's as if with any turn I take, she will be around the corner. I stop myself, trying to get a grip on reality.

"Everything all right?" asks Bronin from behind me.

"Yes. I'm fine." That's when I look up and notice the paintings on the wall .

"We probably shouldn't wander off from each other," says Bronin standing next to me. I see him eyeing the paintings. "If the castle's changing, we might get separated again."

I hardly hear Bronin, for the painting, crudely nailed to its wood backing, captivates me. It is of a cottage in the woods, surrounded by lush oakburn trees and rooted hills. A paddle wheel on the side of the house sits positioned at the base of a river. It's not the depiction that entrances me, however. It's the picture itself. It seems alive. The wheel spins in the rush of the river, the leaves sway in the blowing wind. It is beautiful, unnatural, and draws me near. What is happening to me? I stop myself and look away. Stepping back, I shake my head. It is pounding, like the heartbeat of an overrun horse. Rubbing my temples, I press on.

The hall is quiet; tiny mice scurry along the rafters as I pass flickering flames. I pass painting after painting, all of them landscapes but different in size. Walking the shadowy passage, I wonder at their meaning. There are so many of them, but one seems to stand out from the rest. Its color, its size. This painting, set in a dark grey wash, is of a large tree. It is dead, removed from any life, sitting alone atop a weeded hill, overlooking a barren meadow.

Like the cottage painting, it captures my interest. Maybe because of its simplicity. Maybe because it stands defiant at the top of a hill. The sound of a rat draws my attention away momentarily. It scurries into a hole across the corridor, back to its haven of security. I feel the energy again. The painting beckoning me. I look up and my blood runs cold.

There are bodies swaying from the branches of the tree. Human bodies. Necks stretched. Eyes bulging. They are fresh. There are women and children, but most of them are men, dressed in the robes of priests. They bump one another like wind chimes blowing in the wind. Something's not right. I need to show Bronin. As I turn to tell him, he is still down the hall by the other painting, leaning forward, running his fingers over the picture.

"Don't!" I call out, raising my hand as if it would stop him.

Dropping his torch, Bronin suddenly lifts from the ground. His hands go to meet his throat. He is gasping for air.

"Bronin!" I yell, running toward him. His face is turning scarlet. Something is strangling him, but there's nothing there. His hands have a grip on something, but I cannot see it. What evil is this? Bronin is staring into the painting; his eyes are wide and full of orange light. I look away and notice the cottage is on fire. The flames look real and I feel the scars on my face aching. I yell out in frustration, trying to pry the invisible fingers from Bronin's air passage. His face is turning blue.

Bronin's hand clasps my arm. He mouths the word "help," but there is no sound.

"I'm trying. I'm trying!" I say, but my strength isn't doing anything. If I use the Bawaka, it might cut him. His eyes begin to waver, then roll upward.

I grab one of the flasks from Bronin's chest and smash it into the painting with my palm. The glass cuts deep into my hand as the liquid splatters over the canvas, mixing water with oil and my blood. A burst of fire ignites instantly and burns the picture of the cottage along with my hand. The fire burns my skin and I scream in agony, twisting my hand harder against the image, insuring its effect. The painting screeches with deafening recourse as if it were alive. The grip on Bronin suddenly breaks and we fall to the floor, Bronin gasping for air, myself clutching my blackened hand. The blisters bubble up quickly, some of them bursting with pus. They hurt so badly I cannot control my teeth from chattering. I inch away from the roaring inferno that once used to be the cottage painting. The fire is hot and I fear it might consume us both if we stay. Bronin coughs, stretching out a hand to communicate he will live. Helping each other, we move quickly past rafters and squealing mice, past paintings I dare not look at, until we reach the end of the hall. Smoke pours from the corridor and out into the large expanse before us. I can hear the flames raging behind. There are multiple screeches now. I have a feeling more of the paintings caught fire.

"Let me see," demands Bronin grabbing the wrist of my blackened hand, the left one where the bracelet used to sit.

Diana, my beautiful love. I am hurting.

My hand is horrible to look at, but Bronin keeps on tending to me, uncorking a leather skin from his satchel, dousing my pustule-covered hand with cold water. The application works and the pain temporarily subsides. "Keep at it. But pour just a little at a time. We need to conserve the water."

I follow his advice as he searches again through his bag.

"You need clean bandages or that will become infected quickly." He pulls out strips of yellowish cloth. "They aren't very clean, but it's all I have." He begins rolling my hand with the thin cloth, stinging my skin. Bronin suddenly erupts into a coughing fit, pausing his application. "Thank you for saving my life," he manages to say, tying off the last of the bandage.

"Don't thank me. Many people died because of me." I try not to think of the plausible outcome. That Dorian might be next.

CHAPTER
XVI

EXPLORING THE DEEP UNDERGROUND OF the ruins does nothing for my pain. My hand hurts more now than before. The bandages are soaked from the water. I keep dripping more on it, yet it doesn't seem to help. Every movement I make seems to bring back the memory of the fire in the painting, the evil energy lurking in the depths of Egleaseon's ruins. More so, I feel irritated from the buzzing sound about the air. I can't place it. The light around me feels unnatural.

Despite the awkward flickering light, I am amazed at the destruction everywhere. Entering into a helpless mess, the court-yard Bronin spoke of was an understatement. Large statues once standing tall lie in ruin, scattered about the ground. Some of them lie on their sides. Mythical beasts, creatures with great furry manes or skin made of serpentine scales. Some I have seen, some I have not. Pots and urns line the walls. They too are subject to the wreckage. Pillars broken off at their bases lie among the rubble of destroyed walls. Odd metal structures stand erect between the ruins of large boulders. Some of them bent, they flash and buzz, flickering on and off, but unlike actual candles. Electricity. I have seen such ingenuity before. Lampposts in Sunstone, the capitol. It is no surprise the count had procured these. He was a collector of artifacts. Expensive ones. Lampposts would be a sure boast and conversation piece.

Sparks ignite from the few broken fixtures, most of the gas, if not all, having escaped its pressurized chambers. The light is bright and I try not to look directly at it. Everything in the chamber is enormous, making it difficult to climb over the material of fallen candelabras and furniture. Ahead, I notice a tree, crushed by a stone hand railing. A fountain spraying water horizontally. Vines and weeds creeping through broken drainage grates.

In some places, rose stems litter the soft dirt. I remember when I brought Diana white roses, told her they symbolized our purity, and she laughed. "We are anything but pure, Tenor." Her voice is so vivid in my mind. My stomach churns as I grip my wrist, the pain is returning to my hand.

Without realizing, I kick something on the ground. A thick book with its pages flipped open. Inside, a flattened rose bud, red as blood, lies wedged in the fold of the binding, perfectly intact. I pick it up and sniff its lingering floral scent. There's no telling how long it has been here, but something strange about it has me perplexed. I knew Egleaseon collected books, but books such as these? Sagas of romance, a collection. *The Dramatis Endeavors of Aria.* Such love-tainted stories. What interest in love did Egleaseon ever have?

I cast the book aside and notice more dried rose stems, a trail of them snaking through chairs and under rubble until they finally lead to a withered rose bush, made to look like a person. It lies on its side with roots exposed, revealing bones that long ago were buried underneath it. A graveyard perhaps? I look up into the black air above, wondering how far the castle stood erect from this very spot, and how many souls were tortured and condemned to die.

In every direction, more bushes stand. Each of them headless in their own way. Thorny and grotesque, crushed by bookcases and fallen stone. This place is devastating, and as I walk through it all, the trail soon becomes nearly impassible.

Using a large rock as a step, I help Bronin over the fallen wreckage of a bookcase. "Don't use the shelves as support," I say, but as the words come out, Bronin's boot crashes through the first of the shelves. Wood snaps and splinters sending moth-eaten books pouring onto the floor.

"Damn it to hell," curses Bronin, kicking off broken wood pieces.

I am stunned. I've never heard Bronin curse before. I see the anger in his face and his eyebrows wrinkle with frustration. Seems I am not the only one the castle is affecting.

Gripping his arm with both hands, I assist in pulling him to his feet, and he clears the bookshelf. Turning around, a breeze blows at my back and I know there is an opening somewhere off in the distance. There has to be a way out, unless the castle came to life again and changed its walls. "Watch your step," I call out to Bronin as I hear him struggling within the wreckage. I leap from overturned bookshelves onto loose stones, moving far ahead of him. He can manage on his own.

Coming to rest aside a lamppost spared from the castle's implosion, I find the metal is warm, channeled with electricity from the aqueducts far below. The buzzing is strong and my hand vibrates. The high-pressure sodium churns in its glass prison above me, its yellow glow dimming and brightening. Somewhere in the distance, I hear the deep bell of a clock, signifying some deranged hour. There are no windows to view the outside. Time is lost to me. Whether it is day or night, as long as I can breathe, I will search for Dorian.

Through the darkness, beyond the yellow light of my torch, I see silver light. The breeze I felt earlier has grown stronger and chills the sweat under my proofing. Following the light, I come to a massive archway, higher than I can see. On either side, gargoyles made of dark grey stone squat by the entrance like sentinels. Long fangs extend from their open mouths like dragons' teeth. Each of their hands clutches a skull of the same stony caliber. Moving closer, I watch their empty eyes, waiting for them to follow me. But they never do. Still, the gargoyles seem so real, I cannot take my eyes off them as I pass by, holding the Bawaka before me in case they might strike.

The archway, riddled with cobwebs, is disturbed through its center, proving someone passed through here recently. A loose stone sends me stumbling into a large room bathed in silver light. Large paintings hang along the walls; balcony after balcony extends upward to reveal floors that once existed. A gold and silver embroidered chandelier hangs from the pinnacle of the ceiling, swaying gently from the whistling of the wind. Spiderwebs droop from it like white sheets. Cautiously I move through the foyer, the grand entryway where Egleaseon received his guests. I remember it well, hundreds of candles lighting the night inside the castle, its condition always immaculate despite the absence of servants.

I come to stand before the great double doors at the castle entrance. There are steps leading down to the driveway. The night is alive; trees thrash about from unseen forces. The tall grasses bristle with ferocity. The howling is so loud, I'm not sure if it's wind passing through branches or willdermen crying at the moon. The door is open enough for a person to pass through, however, and so I use the weight of my body to push it shut. On impact, large pane windows high above rattle, sending fragments of glass showering down around me.

It is very quiet in the foyer with the wind suppressed. The familiar buzz of the electric lamp fizzles from an overhead globe, the color of milky brown. Moths peck at it ominously with no direction, confused from the artificial light. There are more like it but none of them work. They are cracked from fallen debris. It's a surprise this one works at all. Long candelabras lie on their sides, scraped from rolling on the floor. Rats scurry through crushed candle wax, trailing bits of white dust throughout the foyer. I watch one scampering away from the rest and my eyes settle on a contraption at the far end of the room. Set between two enormous staircases, brass tubes rise from a wooden frame, bent and frayed at the ends. The organ reminds me of the one at Albestan Church, the one Bronin played. The one Nestor was supposed to be playing before he died.

I approach it cautiously as if the construct were alive. I'm not sure why I hold my hand out to it, maybe to feel something, energy perhaps. But I sense nothing, except the dull stale air of the room. The breeze has gone and warmth is finally returning to me. Moving closer, I see that some of the keys are missing and the stool used for sitting is gone. Like the rest of the room, the organ is coated with ghostly cobwebs. Tiny spiders creep their way about the manuals, disappearing in and out of cracks spreading from the stops. I remember the keys playing by themselves from my previous visit, some trick of Egleaseon's. Now they remain motionless, caked in dust.

Bronin appears next to me, eyeing the instrument as I do. His hand runs along the frame of the wooden box, leaving trails in the thick dust. His face is solemn. Maybe he is thinking of Nestor, the boy who was coming of age. Nestor was his prodigy, the son he would never have, and the next in line to master the duties of the head priest. Bronin was to move up the ranks, become part of the high order, one of Archbishop Faeradon's confidants. But all that has changed now.

Bronin's hand suddenly falls to the keys on one of the manuals and a horrific blast of air issues from the pipes. The sound resonates through the room and everything around me vibrates. Glass falls from the windows, crystals tinkle from the chandelier. And then there is a sudden burst from behind the organ. A cloud of dust emanates as a swarm of bats pours from the underbelly of the contraption.

Grabbing Bronin, I force him down to the ground as the bats frenzy about the chamber, shrieking and flapping their wings, causing the pressure in my veins to escalate.

"Cover yourself!" I shout, hoping Bronin hears me through the chaos. Before I am able to do the same, the bats, in synch, swoop into a circle, pass my face, and exit the foyer through a missing window. They disappear just as they quickly as they appear. I feel the heart in my chest thumping against the floor and my hand burns with pain. I need more water to soak the bandage.

Bronin is breathing fast next to me. For a moment, I think he might be dying, but as I sit up I see him clutching his chest, trying to calm his breathing.

I cannot stop the frustration I feel at the moment. "What were you thinking? Everything in the castle knows we're here now."

I watch Bronin's eyeballs twitch about in all directions. I give him a good shake despite my blistering hand. "Wake up!"

Bronin looks into my eyes. "Lord Wolfgang—I'm so sorry," he whispers.

"Why did you do that?" My words are harsh, despite the terror on his face.

"I—I'm not sure—I felt compelled to touch it."

"We are searching for Joachim," I say, squeezing my fists with every passing moment. "And now he will know we're here."

A scream echoes down the stairwell.

My heart stops.

Up in an instant, I dash for the stairs. There is a bright light coming from the top. Each step is an effort, as I climb over broken stones. Collapsed walls have dashed away parts of the stairs. I leap over gaping holes and missing ledges, all the while my mind racing. I cannot squeeze the Bawaka any tighter in my hand. Thoughts and images flood my mind; all that I will do to Joachim when I see him.

Nearing the summit, I pause, hearing another wretched scream. This time, a voice follows.

"Please—Please, I beg you. Don't—" the voice chokes.

A second voice follows, high in pitch, yet ragged and full of rasp. "And so the king, thinking it was owed to him, he, a man of great standard and stock, took what was precious from the little girl."

The words make me uncomfortable and I slow my advance. Neither voice is Joachim's or Dorian's.

"Please, don't—" the first voice asks, weaker this time.

I hear the sound of liquid spilling onto the floor.

"He took everything from the little girl," continues the second voice. "Because he could. It's what kings do. Take things. Wouldn't you agree?"

There is more choking followed by a moan.

"I think so," the second voice replies to itself. "And do you know what the king did next?"

Looking back, I see Bronin making his way toward me. My finger goes to my lips.

"He made good use of the blood between her legs."

CHAPTER
XVII

MOVING PAST THE RAILINGS OF the stairs, I take shelter behind a bookcase. The second-floor balcony is full of them, against the walls and next to tables. The bright light hurts my eyes. Melted candles cover every surface of what's left of a library. I cannot see the talking figure with the raspy voice. The bookcases are too dense with books.

"The blood, you see," continues the raspy voice, "is the essence of power." Whimpering comes from another person in the room.

I sense Bronin is about to say something and shake my hand to silence him. The look on his face is confounded. He is bending to see through the books like me.

"And without power, you see, one becomes useless."

I need a better position. Edging up to the side of the bookcase, I angle my head just enough to see a figure in a black cloak, bent over an open book, busily scribbling away with a feather pen. Scars trace its lips.

"*Useless* is unacceptable." There is a pause. "Fortune favors you, my friend. You are not useless." The figure chuckles.

I move from one bookcase to another, using the shadows from the towering shelves to hide my body. Crouching at the knees, beams of light fall on my face through the cracks between the books. I position myself for a better look.

"And the moral of the story is?"

I see who the figure is speaking to. A bearded man, stripped to nothing but a laborer's pants. Tattered cloth hangs from his skin at bloodied parts of his torso. Sitting in a chair with his arms outstretched across the table, the underside of his arms face up, exposing deep lacerations in his taught skin. Eyes closed, his head sways around on his shoulders, bobbing around like a doll. The figure in the cloak stops writing and paces around the tortured man, carrying the pointed object he was writing with.

"Power is everything," the figure says, clasping the man by his hair.

Exposing his hand from underneath the cloak, the captor holds it up to the prisoner's face. There are black nails, long like daggers, protruding from his fingertips.

In an instant they are in the man's arm, filleting his flesh like a specimen in a laboratory. The man, unable to move his head, screams horribly. Tears run down his face; blood drips from his missing teeth. The chains binding him rub raw at the wrists, exposing a portion of bone in his forearm. More blood streams from the ripped scabs. "Please, I beg you," says the tortured man. I can barely hear him. The black-cloaked figure brandishes the feather pen and dips it into the freshly made cut. The man screams again as the figure moves back to his book and begins writing with fresh blood.

I run my finger over the blade of the Bawaka. Enough of this.

I stand to approach but Bronin gets in my way, stopping me as I did him. "Don't," he whispers. "What if it sees us?"

"Sees who?" responds the raspy voice.

Bronin closes his eyes. The hairs on my arm tingle.

More chuckling follows. "You can come out now. I've entertained long enough."

I step out from the shadows holding the Bawaka before me like a sword. The bearded man's eyes widen from my sudden appearance. "Lord Wolfgang, please—help me!" The man can barely talk.

"Lord Wolfgang is it?" asks the cloaked figure. I see within the shadow of his hood a pale face and sunken eyes. Slender white hands. Long nails.

Bronin appears beside me with a flask in his hand.

"And a cohort. Seems an introduction is in order since we are all here." The cloaked figure motions to the man in the chair and to some random location behind him. Looking past his shoulders, I cannot comprehend the horror I see.

An iron cage braced on a stand holds thin naked people stuffed inside, like sausages in a butcher's box. No room to move, the flat bars press against their arms and legs. Their skin is pulled taut over ribs; obviously they haven't eaten in weeks. A woman. A child. Two men. Their yellow eyes stare beyond me. Lost. Forgotten.

"I am the master librarian, Roul, and these obedient servants you see here have graciously volunteered their time, aiding me in my research." Roul smiles.

"Release them!" I say, stepping forward.

The people in the cage startle at the sound of my voice.

"I am master of this castle, not you," says Roul, looking about the walls and shelves, "What's left of it."

"You are not the master. I killed him long ago!"

"Is that so?"

Before I can react, Roul digs his nails inside the man's arms again, twiddling his fingers.

The man screams.

"Stop!" I say, taking another step.

"You can make it stop," says Roul, twisting his fingers deeper into the meat of the man's muscles. "Or make it worse." The man shakes as blood spurts onto the table.

I feel useless. Retaliation will cost the man's life. My hand is numb from squeezing the Bawaka. My eyes dart about the room.

"Good," says Roul. "Lord Wolfgang possesses reason. That is rare for a hunter." He smiles and nods his head approvingly. "I never finished my story." He gestures with his hand and the book he was writing in comes soaring to him. Dipping the quill into the man's arm, he begins writing. "Now, where were we? Ah yes, since we established his power is everything, the king strived to ensure he would never lose it again."

My focus is elsewhere. There are tapestries hanging from every wall, curtains from every archway.

"And since blood is power, and all of the girl's blood was used, he didn't simply throw her away. Oh no, he still had use for her. There is another element in power to consider."

To the back of the chamber, on either side, there are halls leading out, one going up and one down. Tall standing candelabras light the way.

"Fear." Roul pauses, dipping his pen in blood again. The bearded man cries out. The cage shakes. The little girl inside moves in response.

Roul scribbles in his book. "Fear, is the second prime element. So the king did what he must."

Roul's words are distracting, penetrating my thoughts. I try not to listen, to force him out. I focus on other things. I notice the woman in the cage is awake.

"On a pale moon night, when the orb was full in its glory, he strung her on the castle wall, split her from the navel to her pretty little parts, and left her for the crows to peck. His subjects knew him. His enemies knew him. God knew him." Roul looks at the ceiling with a smile.

There is precious little time.

"Roul," I shout, "Have you seen a boy and a man?"

Roul turns his head to me. "Changing the subject, I see. Brash," he says with pointed teeth. "Very well. I have seen no boy, only a man. He is with the Carnalreesee." His lips curl at the edges as he chuckles.

The Carnalreesee. The chosen of Egleaseon's closest. They should have perished after the castle fell. I want to ask more questions about them but suddenly, the cage behind Roul begins moaning. All the people inside are awake and alert. I see their arms reaching out, grasping at the air, feet dangling like worms. More moans come. The little girl's lips are trembling.

"Please help me," the man in the chair says, struggling with every phrase. I hear the fresh blood in his windpipe.

"Oh, this is too dramatic," says Roul, lashing out with a hand, cutting the man's neck. Blood sprays onto the table and book, speckling Roul's face red.

"No!" I shout over Roul's sinister laughter.

"Look at you making me waste perfectly good blood," says Roul, wiping his face and licking his fingers. "How will I finish my stories now?"

Red liquid pours from the man's neck like a fountain.

"With your blood I suppose," finishes Roul casually.

The Bawaka leaves my hand. Spinning through the air with such speed, Roul is gone before the blade reaches him.

"Back! Now!" I say to Bronin as my blade comes whirling into my hand. A blurred image passes back and forth toward me. Instinctively, I raise the Bawaka before my face, bracing it with both hands. Roul's teeth lash onto the center, his fangs grind on the leather wrapped handle, inches away from my face. I see the black of his sunken eyes. Blue capillaries spread across his face as his jaw tenses against the cross shape of the Bawaka.

He grabs both of my arms and lifts me from the ground with ease, tossing me into a bookcase. My body breaks every shelf on the way down, splintering wood and scattering books. My teeth rattle as my head hits the ground. A cascade of leather-bound volumes falls around me as I struggle to upright myself.

A burst of fire across the room sets me in motion. The fire is hot and burns away a bookshelf riddled with old parchments and vials. Some of them pop as I approach, crouching, trying to keep below the visible height of the chairs and tables. I splash through what I think is water, then realize it's not water. Red and thick, all of the blood has drained from the dead man in the chair. Head tilted to the side, he gazes at me with a lifeless stare.

Where is Bronin?

Desperately I search, scanning the ground, the shelves. The smoke makes my eyes burn. Something passes before me. "Bronin!" I shout. There is no response. The fire is traveling up the walls along old tapestries, igniting instantly. It seems the entire room is ablaze.

It passes by me again and stops before a stone vase spared from destruction. Roul stands erect with his arms at his sides, nails fanned out like fins. He waits a moment, watching me as if contemplating something. He says nothing. Slowly he begins walking toward me and then, like a flash of lighting, he comes quickly, moving side to side with precision, his image distorting in the process. Nails swipe at my face. I step back. A thrust to my abdomen. I parry the blow then cut. His fragile skin opens at the wrist, spraying blood across papers and flames. Without regard, he swipes at me again, this time with both his hands, one at my head, one at my torso. I have no choice but to protect my face as his other hand rakes my chest, shredding the proofing like tree bark.

Using his momentum, I grip his black cloak and roll onto my back, thrusting with my leg. Roul flies through a pillar, breaking apart stone and ripping sconces from the wall. Stone comes crumbling down around him, crushing his body.

I hear crying in the distance. Rubbing my eyes, it's nearly impossible to see anything with all the smoke. In a brief moment, I see the cage turned on its side over a pile of splintered wood.

"Lord Wolfgang," comes a feeble voice.

It's the little girl.

Choking through the smoke, I struggle toward her.

"Lord Wolfgang," comes another voice, female yet stronger.

How do they know my name? They must be villagers from Roland.

Suddenly, my head snaps back. Pain shoots through my skull as fingers rip at my hair.

"I think not," says Roul, his stinking breath on my face. High above us there is a wooden chandelier covered in fire. "Look at this! Look what you've done!" Roul screams, nearly bursting my eardrum. "All of my work! Wasted!" His grip tightens; the tips of his nails break the surface of my skin. He is going to crush my skull.

Where the hell are you, Bronin?

Screams come from the cage. Roul jerks my head in its direction. The little girl's eyes are crinkled and closed. The iron bars are burning into her skin like a cattle brand. She screams and doesn't stop. Tears stream down my face. Anger and hatred well up inside me.

"Look at all that good stock going to waste," Roul says; I hear the blood rattling in his lungs. "Lucky I have you."

There is cold, moist air on my neck, and I know what is coming. My jaw tenses, my eyes flick open. Fire is everywhere, consuming everything. The heat irritates the scars on my face. The cage is consumed in the fire. The moaning has stopped. I cannot break free of Roul's death grip.

There is a loud groan high above. The walls rumble. The pain in my head suddenly lessens. An opportunity.

With upward force, I bring my elbow into Roul's chest, enough to distract him for a moment. Grabbing his hand, I slice it off with the Bawaka. Its sharp edge cuts through flesh and bone, severing every decayed tendon in the vampire's wrist. I tumble forward, roll on the ground through burning books and turn to face Roul with determination. He will no longer write with that pen.

Eyes wide. Roul screams. "Bastard! My hand! My hand!"

But he doesn't scream for long.

The groan high above is followed by the snapping of a chain and the chandelier comes crashing down, burying Roul beneath a tomb of burning splinters. I hear moaning beneath the fiery grave and relish at his suffering. His cries are nothing to me. I watch the last moments of his existence turn to ash.

CHAPTER
XVIII

DEBRIS CONTINUES TO FALL.

Burning tapestries. Burning wood. Fire has made everything unstable, heating all things flammable from the inside out. Paintings blacken in their frames. Balconies break from their foundations. Fire is everywhere, yet Bronin is nowhere. The smell of roasted flesh makes my stomach churn. My eyes fall on the cage that held the villagers. Consumed in fire, the iron bars glow vibrant orange. I close my eyes, trying to banish the memory of the girl's skin blistering, the others inside, crammed against her, shouting in her tiny ears.

Coughing takes over and I gag. Bile rises to my mouth. The smoke is black and thick. I need to leave or I will suffocate to death. The stairs are somewhere back here. They lead downward. Somewhere.

I cover my face, passing row after row of burning shelves. Despite knowing this place will collapse any minute, Roul's rhetoric lingers inside me, a voice I will never forget. He said a man passed through here, not a boy. I panic at the thought it might be too late, that Joachim has already killed Dorian, disposed of my son's body in some desolate tomb, or worse. I cannot think of such things, but I have failed innocent people again. I could not protect the ones in the cage. Death mocks my every step and yet, something new seems to take hold over me. This inner obsession I cannot comprehend. I remember years ago, teaching Dorian in the courtyard of Wolfgang Manor the ways of the sword, that even when dealing the killing blow to your enemy, always do so with confidence. Serve justice. Not malice. And yet with each step I descend into this new darkness, I am overcome with the presence of evil. Not just any evil. Revenge.

Joachim has taken everything from me. I, the one who took him in at the same age as Dorian presently is, and this is my return payment. With Bronin gone, I feel God is further from me than ever before. Everything that ever was holy, that kept me glued together, was Bronin. Not now, not anymore. He has burned away in the fire with the rest of the victims.

Yes, revenge. My newfound strength. When I find Joachim, before I do what must be done, he will show me Dorian's body. I will not let my son rot away in this forsaken place. He will have a proper burial, a funeral pyre like his mother's, to ensure his purity to heaven.

I wipe away tears as I reach for a candelabra. I am not surprised that it is lit. Joachim has come this way. The stairs are long in descent. The glow of the candles flickers in the corridor. The further I go, the darker it gets. The atmosphere has become cooler again, frigid almost, and my body shivers. Skulls rest in orifices cut out in the walls. Ornamentation common throughout Egleaseon's castle. I always wondered about the ironic memento moris he placed everywhere, that he of all vampires would dream of death constantly. Such a tortured state Egleaseon had been in. The image of him gripping the Hand of God, his body glowing white, will never leave my memory.

A tremor sounds off in the distance. I keep walking, ignoring the many others that follow, indignant and indifferent about whether I live or die. Funny how revenge trumps all reason, and that I go about it so willingly.

I'm not sure how long I travel the looming passage, passing door after door, all of them locked and covered in dust. They must lead somewhere, but I don't have the strength to break them down. I keep going; forward being the only option. Along the walls, collections of art decorate the way. Sculptured busts I've never seen before, fancy porcelain vases painted with black and red patterns, tapestries that drape all the way to the ground. A clock comes into view that maybe rose to the ceiling at one point in time. Now, shattered at its center, the top portion lies on its side, toppled over from the cave-in all around it. Rubble and wood fill the interior of its body like pebbles collected in a jar. Lizards and beetles with hard-shelled backs rummage through the wreckage, pushing sand and silt aside, scavenging for smaller prey. I wonder what grotesque thing waits underneath it all. The smell is unbearable. Crunching over a centipede, I bring myself closer to the clock's face, admiring the framework of dark wood and metal used for the enormous hands. The glass used to protect the face is shattered into thousands of pieces, making it difficult to read the time. Tilting my head to the side, I see the smaller hand is almost on the four, the big hand approaching the twelve. Moving closer still, I position myself to angle my ear just right. I hear ticking inside. Impossible.

Quickly I step back, looking all around, preparing for a trap, but there is nothing but the crawling of insects and the clock's clicking. I stare at the broken frame. The pendulum used to power the clock lies bent and mangled on the ground.

The big hand suddenly moves over the twelve position with a heavy click. I wait for some bell to tone even though there is none and nothing happens. Then, immediately following, the walls and ground begin shaking and vibrating with such force, I crouch low to stabilize myself. The noise is deafening. Insects dart between cracks, worms squirm through rotted wood. I wonder if the tremor from before was the same as this. Cracks form under my boots. One races between my legs and I suddenly have the urge to run, but can't.

Instead, I fall, reaching for edges, grasping at anything available. The floor splits beneath my feet, candlesticks disappearing into a huge abyss below. My hands find an earthen root; it peels from the soil like the unthreading of a cloak, bursting black dirt from the ground and then snapping. Dirt stings my face and I squint back the burning in my eyes. I can't hold on any longer. Down into darkness I descend, the earth consuming me. The light of the passage above becomes smaller and smaller until there is no more light with which to see.

CHAPTER
XIX

THE ABSENCE OF LIGHT. PITCH black.

It is the first time I recall falling while remaining conscious. As I speedily descend, I cannot see my arms and hands desperately clawing at the moist soil around me. My face is tortured, battered by roots and rocks, terrible pain against the scars below my eye and the blisters on my hand. My boots find some resistance, spreading wet dirt like a plow on a farm. I slow some but momentum keeps me endlessly spinning. Something is chasing after me through the pit, gaining speed, coming closer. I hear its whistling, its roar as it ricochets off the walls. I grind my teeth at the thought of contact.

Unexpectedly, my legs buckle. I flip over onto my stomach, slide through worms and larvae and come to stop. Clenching my fists, cold wet soil full of granules mashes between my fingers. A strong draft blows from somewhere above me. My muscles tense. Metal and glass explode all around me. The sounds of springs twanging and wood snapping. The noise makes my ears ring. More things fall around me—pebbles, rocks, even a boulder I think. I scramble backwards in fear of being crushed to death and wait in the darkness. My head throbs. I shake it, trying to regain my senses. Then I remember the candles.

I grope through the blackness, praying my hands find the things that will save me from this eternal dark. And then I feel them. Thin sticks of wax, and the bent and twisted remnants of the candelabra. I make do with the instruments of light, placing the candles in their odd directions. Reaching into my satchel, my fingers grip the rough flint stone and dried moss used for sparking fires. The first hit against stone causes me to flinch from the bright flash. I do it again, catching the moss and then a small flame ignites.

Splintered wood and metal gears lie all around me as if I'm in an abandoned junkyard. I shudder at seeing my surroundings. Glass sparkles in the candlelight as I crunch around the destruction. Everything is obliterated from the heavy impact. The wood casing. The interior of the pendulum box. The only thing left resembling a clock is the iron hands used to tell time. With one end pointing out of the ground, I stare at it, waiting for it to move. All is quiet.

Looking around the chamber in the glow of candlelight, I find it difficult to make out anything. Shadows cast to and fro, wavering on the walls like specters, forcing me to flinch at my own shadow with the Bawaka in hand. If only there was more light. Progression is slow and daunting. The room smells of a deep, rich earth, like leaves soaked in rainwater. But there is another scent. The smell of rotting death.

Unexpectedly, I lurch forward, nearly falling flat on my face. A quick sweep with the candles reveals my boot wedged between two cobblestones. With a tug, my boot is free and I immediately take notice of a stone structure in the dim light. It is cold against my fingertips as I run my hand the length of the top. Realizing it is a tomb covered in greyish dirt, I back away quickly, keeping my distance. I can see things crawling along its surface, uncertain if the candles are playing tricks on my eyes. Spiderwebs droop to the floor, blowing gently from some unknown breeze. Strange. I don't feel a draft.

Close by, I hear the trickling of dirt against the tomb and cobblestones. I dare not linger. Even though I am surrounded by death, this place feels alive. I hold the candles high over my head, attempting the best angle of light. The flames flicker, almost blowing out. They recover. I exhale.

There is a rumble off in the distant, but as the tremor subsides, more follow. I am at the mercy of structural integrity. Any moment this underground place could collapse in on itself, burying me along with any hope of finding my son. But the ground calms and I press on ever slowly, darkness hindering my progression. The underground tunnel system is vast with interlocking chambers. The cavity I fell into seems to have no end—until my hand grips fresh soil. The dirt is black in the candlelight, glistening from the moisture as it slips from my palm.

Sweeping the candelabra back and forth, I notice head-sized objects protruding from the wall. They are skulls, dozens of them, maybe hundreds.

Row upon row, they line the walls in every direction, disappearing from my circle of light. Wedged in the dirt like ornaments of a palace, they vary from small to large. All the while I imagine to whom they had belonged. I walk farther, gazing at the dead, reaching an area narrowing into a crowded hall. A hall not populated by people or furniture, but tombs. They line the base of the hall, side by side, stretching farther than my eyes can see. Above them, resting on shelves carved from the soil, are wooden coffins. The smell of earth has long surpassed the stench of death in this decrepit place, evidence to how ancient my surroundings are. Wiping cobwebs away, I find a coffin dated more than a thousand years old. It's an interesting notion, walking among the dead servants of Egleaseon's lineage spanning thousands of years. What have these walls seen?

I pass more tombs dated later than the one before, during the time of the Revelation, when vampires first emerged publicly over two thousand years ago. I wonder at the contents within the caskets. Heirlooms, paintings—things vampires never part with. Even in death the lesson of life is never achieved.

I keep to the center of the corridor, avoiding any contact with the tombs. My boots echo as I progress. Back and forth my eyes dart, watching skulls and coffins pass by. There are so many. As I realize I'm trapped in the catacombs, a horrible feeling, one of sickness and desolation, comes over me, for I am the closest one can be to hell. I shudder at the thought of dead spirits hissing and clawing at my flesh, molesting my body, yet unable to literally touch me. Yet.

There is a gust of cold air again and I stop, hearing a faint whisper, but it passes from one ear to the next. A distorted sound, disembodied in nature, as if whatever is making the sound is struggling to get the words out. The hairs on my ears prickle. I turn my head, but nothing's there.

A long drawn out word whispers through the hall. "Thisssssssssssss."

I try to look beyond the blackness of the hall, keeping the candles placed behind my head to prevent the glare. "Hello?" I say, testing my sanity.

A cool breeze blows against my face, caressing me like a soft hand. No, could it be . . . ? I struggle to banish the thought from my mind, but the idea saturates me like an unforgettable stain. How I've missed Diana. All this death surrounding me amplifies my desire for her. I see her pale face lying on the dirt in the courtyard. I clench my eyes shut. "Diana?" I manage to say, choking on my speech.

"Tenor," comes the disembodied voice. Through the stale air, I make out the tenderness of a woman's speech.

"Diana, is that you?" I can't help thinking she's here with me. So long she's plagued my dreams, raptured my body, I can't pass up the chance to be in her presence.

There is a light, silver like the moon, twirling around the base of a tomb, and it spins off to a new location. It passes from one tomb to the next, like an iridescent snake floating off the ground. It's trail leaves behind a mist of smoke, dissipating just as quickly as it appears.

"Come, Tenor," the whisper beckons.

I follow despite my better judgment. Reason is lost to me. My heart pounds beneath my breastbone. A few steps, and my foot brushes one of the tombs. Tremors rattle the walls of the narrow passage, shaking loose dirt from the ceiling. There is a tremendous crash behind me. When I turn around, there is no fire, no heat. Only the remains of a long-dead servant sprawled across the floor. One of the coffins has fallen from the wall, breaking apart like a mangled crate. The skull at the head of the body stares at me, its mouth open, as if lamenting in silence. Around its neck a brass oval pendant lies tangled in its own chains. Hollow eyes stare at me as I reach down, open the pendant, and wipe the dust from the glass. There is a picture of a man and woman, side by side, proper and elegant with black faded clothing.

I look over my shoulder, but the light has vanished. The disembodied voice echoes from the hall, as if moving away. I do not know what it is saying. "Diana. I am coming." Dropping the pendant, I run down the corridor, watching for loose stones and cracks in the floor.

There it is, the light—it twists deep into the dark hall, only to vanish again. My pulse quickens, as I fear I might lose her. Reaching a turn in the hall, I somewhat calm myself, realizing she hasn't left me after all. She is passing along skulls and cobwebs, cracked tombs and gnarled roots. Everything I walk past sparkles in the whitish glow. Diana. *Wait for me.*

She passes above crosses and tombstones. There are epitaphs scrawled across every rock her light touches. The atmosphere becomes lighter. High above there are cracks of light piercing through the abysmal darkness. Is it day or night? I've lost track of time. I come bursting into a vast chamber full of rich history. An underground graveyard. Catacomb walls stretch higher than the light allows me to see. Skulls and coffins reach up to the very heavens. I stop running and hold my breath.

Before me lies a structure made of old mossy stone. Eight pillars surround the outer edge of a raised floor. Steps lead up to its center, a rotunda, similar to the one where Diana and I used to meet when we were young. Everything is as it was then, except for the immense rock smashed through the backside of the roof. Half of the rotunda is gone, crushed among pebbles. Could it be the very one from Delore?

The voice whispers around my head. "Tenor."

I move past gravestones along the path drawn by Diana's shimmering iridescent light. There is an impatient breath. "Tenor."

"I'm coming, my love."

It is strange approaching the rotunda, centered in a valley of death and stone. Maybe I'm not awake. Maybe I'm dreaming. Maybe I'm dead.

A chill passes through me and I rub my eyes. Regardless of what is real or not, I continue because my angel is calling me. I must go to her. As I ascend the stairs, I feel no imminent threat, and lower my hands.

Standing at the center of a large circle, I look around at the smooth marble floor. My reflection stares at me through centuries of dust. The slivers of light from high above show my pale complexion.

Am I dead?

"Tenor, come to me," sighs Diana's voice. I imagine her soft breath on my neck, the way her speech muffled in my hair when I pulled her close.

But there is nothing now, except the vast emptiness all around me. I am like the sun at the center of a barren universe. No planets. No stars. My eyes are wide with hope as I go from one pillar to the next, searching for something, anything. I wipe back tears hearing her voice very near.

"Don't cry, my Lord Wolfgang."

My blood runs cold as I turn to see Diana standing behind me. Perfect in form, her image is solid and white, brighter than the evening star and her eyes like two black holes. What words do I have to say except, "D." I step forward and she steps back, raising her arms.

"Don't, Tenor."

I want to touch her, embrace her. I take another step.

"No," she says assertively.

"But why?" I am lost to all thought. I am alive. Blood pumps through my veins.

"Do you remember the spot?" she asks. "Where you used to hold me?" Her figure moves to the edge of the rotunda, gazing out over the vast field of graves. Her hands rest against the railing, but not really.

"Of course I do," I say, rubbing at my wrist where the leather used to be.

"It was much like this one. Bleak. Riddled with cold stones."

I don't understand why she's telling me this. I come up behind her, to embrace her, how I so wantonly desire her touch. I hear her drawing breath. A shudder. I reach to cast her long black hair from her back, to expose the fleshy white softness of her neck.

But my hand passes through her and she vanishes in a puff of white smoke. I stagger forward, gripping the railing where her tender hand was. The surface is cold. I try to choke back the swelling in my eyes.

"You chose me, Tenor," says Diana's voice from behind me. It sounds hollow and emotionless.

I don't want to look. "Yes, I chose you. And I have failed you. Why do you torment me so, haunting my visions day and night?" I wait, yet there's no answer. "Why?" I yell.

"Because you still have purpose, Tenor Alvadine Wolfgang."

I cannot remember the last time she called me by my full name. I knew it meant she was determined, and that she would get what she desired. Always.

"What do you want?" I say, tears dripping from my face. I want to look at her, but can't. The anticipation of touching her one last time has broken me. "Curse this castle!" I scream, kicking the banister. Pieces of stone chip away, falling onto the gravestones below. Turning around, I sink to the floor, my elbows resting on my knees, my face in my hands. I don't want to look. I know she is there, sitting before me. A wind brushes against my skin. I open my eyes and her black eyes are staring at me.

"What do you want," I ask again, unable to control myself.

"For you to save Dorian," she whispers.

I feel dumbfounded by her request. "I have been. It's all I think about." Did I miss something?

Her voice is weak all of a sudden. It wavers, due to some unseen force. "You don't understand, Tenor."

"Wait, don't leave," I say desperately. Despite my anguish, I want her here beside me, even if she's not real. I need her strength. I need her guidance.

There is a tremor off in the distance.

"I did what I could to save him," she says, voice fading. It is nearly gone. I choke on words and struggle to find something to say. But they elude me, as does she.

"Now it's your turn."

I am left to hear nothing but the slight breeze blowing from the high cracks in the cavern ceiling above. Diana is gone.

CHAPTER
XX

THE GROUND BEGINS SHAKING AGAIN, and the pillars of the rotunda start to trickle dust.

I move away, descending the stairs with haste, unsure if the place will come crashing down. I do not know where to go. Diana's spirit guided me this far and now she is gone. I stand in a field of tombstones like a scarecrow lost to the crows of its cornfield.

Another thunderous explosion.

The air becomes thick with dust. I cover my mouth and nose, breathing through the cracks of my fingers, choking, gagging. I dare not look back as I break into a full run. A tombstone to my left explodes; stones shatter away from it. I break to the right and the ground cracks, trailing along the floor, quicker than I can move. I won't fall again.

I leap as the ground crumbles away, just enough to clear the chasm. Tumbling through rocks and frayed roots, I catch my breath as I keep running through the growing dust cloud.

The ground stops shaking yet I keep running, my boots crunching loudly in the temporary silence. My gut churns. Something isn't right. Running only gets me so far.

I am thrown to the ground like a doll. I feel the earth rising up over itself as if I were on top of a giant platform, balancing on a sharp point. Swaying from side to side, I grab a gravestone, stopping myself from sliding. As the cavern floor rises on one side, the other dips down, sending rocks and stones tumbling past me. I feel a thunderous boom close by. It travels through my body, vibrating my bones. Looking over my shoulder, I cringe. A stone pillar twists and turns its way toward me, smashing through gravestones.

Impact. The repercussion of stone on stone jars my clenched teeth and I am forced to let go. The platform is like a plate held to a giant's mouth, tipped to make the food go down faster. I slide, twisting down the platform toward the dark opening, knowing my death is near.

Descending, I wonder if this was all a trap, an illusion to distract me. I see Diana hovering before me, falling with me. Her beautiful glowing figure stays by my side but she is staring out into nothing. I hold out my arms to touch her yet she has no reaction. They simply pass through her. Her body dissipates into smoke. Goodbye, my love—I was able to see your face one last time.

Suddenly, my legs hit something solid and they buckle, sending me into an endless spin. My face strikes a hard surface and a streak of light flashes before me. I hit something again and a rib breaks. What little air I have left in my lungs cries out in pain.

Eventually my tumble into darkness comes to a rough stop. My hands break through pieces of wood and my knees scrape against an uneven floor.

Coughing and choking, I can barely breathe. Not like the ice-cold river from before, but from the condensed dust swarming around my face. It lingers like a cloud full of plague with nowhere to dissipate. I feel the particles tickling the bronchi in my lungs. I cough again and again.

Nothing but pitch black. My body is bruised and sore, but I feel everything is in working order. With no possible way of creating light, I am as good as dead. I sit in silence, listening to the last of the catacomb floor falling all around me. Rocks echo off one another. Sand sliding along stone. Dirt hits me in the face. As I move, rubble falls off me as if I was buried alive. My lungs wheeze with each breath. Everything is cold and grainy in my hands until I come across what feels like a skull. I run my fingers along the teeth and realize some of them are sharp and pointed.

Tossing it aside, I crawl through the darkness directionless; passing what I think is a narrow opening. All of the debris around me is stacked precariously. I know the wrong kind of movement could set off an avalanche, burying me alive. I hold my breath and slide on my side like a worm, wincing at the pressure on my rib. I pull myself through the small hole and my breathing becomes easier. I hear rocks grinding together and know I have to keep moving. Something groans and a thunderous boom follows, shaking the small hole I just came through.

My hand shovels through loose stone, using more muscle than intended. Loose rock tumbles down, entrapping my arm. Jarring pain shoots the course of my ribs. My teeth clench, but I let no sound escape my lips. The thundering settles behind me, and all goes quiet. The sound of moaning breaks through the dull silence. It reminds me of the aqueducts when I first entered the bowels of the ruins. I hear not one, but many, and the noise becomes louder and louder. How fitting all this is, trapped among the dead like a piece of meat.

There is flickering light in the distance, not yellow and orange like flames of fire, but white. Hope ignites my veins. "Diana!" I call out, reaching with my free hand, realizing what I've just done. My voice echoes off the rocks like a man fallen down a well.

The undead moans intensify.

I pull at my arm to break free but it is stuck fast. "Come on," I say to myself, pushing rocks aside and kicking with my leg. Suddenly the light comes to me as if listening to my thoughts, swirling before my face, allowing me to see better.

I keep pulling.

Inches from my face, the head of a lecher snaps its mouth at me. Teeth rubbing together, sinewy tendons exposed, it cannot move any other part of its body. Worms wiggle from its hollow nose and its film-covered eyes roll around without purpose. It makes hissing sounds with its mouth. I strain my neck to look ahead of me. There are more of them, trapped and stuck like this one, buried under rubble, their bodies arrested. They see me and moan uncontrollably. I've been buried alive.

The light continues to taunt me, dancing around my face, teasing me like a trapped animal. Then, one by one, it passes the cadaver heads, causing their white eyes to follow the light. I try again with my arm and this time, it comes loose. I begin crawling after the light, passing rotten teeth and groans. The lechers are not happy. Their meal is getting away. Adrenaline pumping, I do not notice the pain in my side anymore. I am focused on my target, the twirling light.

Dust swirls off me as I emerge from the rubble like a ghost. I stagger through the dim light of my new surroundings, a place of natural stone and stalagmites. They are immense in size, with smooth formations. From their tips, water drips up instead of down, hitting the low ceiling. Moving water is near. I hear it. I stagger a few paces and collapse at the edge of an underground stream. My throat screams for water, but I dare not drink. I can only think this water source stems from the Faust River. I remember what happened the last time it entered my veins. The hallucinogenic powers. The insanity. The price to pay to quench one's thirst. The water looks cool to the touch and I want to dip my burnt hand in the water. I know I can't though. The water effects even open wounds. I dare not chance becoming a victim again. I need every ounce of awareness intact if I am to survive.

I realize the Will-o'-the-wisp has vanished from sight, yet the room remains lit. The light is dim and the color has changed. White to yellow. I take a few moments to collect myself. Where

I am in this vast subterranean world, I do not know. Glancing at the river, it ends abruptly, disappearing into the cavern wall. I wonder how far the system travels underground. My eyes settle on a cave opening concealed by stalagmites. The yellowish glow seems to be coming from there. I slip through the stalagmites with caution. What sort of thing would be waiting for me, I am not sure. Glaring around the corner, there is a passage snaking back and forth. The light is much brighter here and the walls glisten with sweat.

A strong scent of burning meat lingers in the air, but not of the favorable kind. The smell is pungent and musty, like that of a forest ferret. Although the air is thick with the smell of cooking game, I feel like I am surrounded by something. I creep along, gagging, attempting to keep my composure. It becomes increasingly difficult as I get closer and closer, swallowing back the bile in my throat. Through the fiery light I make out a human-like figure, hunched over an open flame, sitting on a large stone. Long straggly hair falls down its back in clumps, dirty and filthy. Next to it, a long piece of wood, fashioned like a spear, rests against its thigh. All around the floor lie dead rats, a dozen or so, mutilated, shredded by something vicious. It is what's over the fire pit cooking that emits the foul odor, a large haunch of meat, from the bottom end of a furless, four-legged creature. My mind has me racing, thinking about the daver hounds. The meaty exposed flesh spits in response to the flames, dripping its rancid juices. Whoever—whatever is tending to the meat, doesn't seem pleased.

The man rubs his hands together, holding them out to the burning meat. "Never warm," he says, pulling at his fingers one by one. "Never warm." His voice is solemn and sarcastic, as if nothing would impress him. After working his hands, he moves on to his wrists and elbows, inching closer to the fire. "And you," the man says addressing the meat over the fire, "look foul and horrid." He stares at it for a moment, then reaches over, stripping off a piece of fleshy meat and shoves it in his mouth. There is a moment of silence. The meat sizzles and the fire crackles as I watch the man chew. Then, he keels over, clutching his abdomen. A moan escapes his lips as he turns on his side, vomiting over rocks and dead rats, grabbing onto what he can. The spear falls over, clattering against the floor, rolling away from his reach.

I position myself closer, keeping to the shadows of the stalagmite formations.

The man calls out. "Why, why me?" he asks, holding his hands out before his face. They are pale and full of veins. I still cannot see his face entirely.

"Why God? What did I do?" Again the man is tormented, bending into the fetal position, writhing on the floor without control.

I move in, positioning myself just behind him where he cannot see me and raise the Bawaka to the back of his neck. I wait for him to stop retching his insides before addressing him.

"Don't move," I say in a low tone.

The man's body tenses from the flat of my blade touching his shoulder.

"Turn around."

He turns to me and his eyes widen, and yet, so do mine.

Pale complexion, dark grey eyes. I stare into the sunken face of Joachim.

CHAPTER
XXI

BEFORE I HAVE A CHANCE to react, Joachim ducks below my blade and rolls away. His movement is fast and strikingly precise, and his hands collect the wooden spear from the ground like a falcon collecting prey. With a swift motion, he thrusts his weapon and I counter, side-stepping his attack. Leaping through the air, he lands on a flat rock next to the fire, pointing his deadly needle at me with malice.

"Bastard, you won't have me this time!" he says. "Begone!"

Joachim's eyes are bloodshot with spider veins spreading from the dark grey of his irises. His shirt is torn in the front of his body and there are stains. Red? Brown? The yellow wash of the firelight makes it impossible to discern.

I merely take a breath and he throws himself at me again, attempting to run his spear through my heart. Catching the shaft of his weapon within the angle of the Bawaka, I send him between two stalagmites as his face strikes the side of the rock.

Blood smears across its surface as he regresses into the shadows, his voice crackling. I want to kill him, right here, right now, but can't. Dorian might be alive and I need answers. I glance around the glowing cave, searching, but Joachim leaps from the shadows, bracing his spear across his chest with both hands, using the weight of his frail looking body. Distraction has cost me my guard.

I can do nothing but collapse onto my back with Joachim's face next to mine. Blood from the gash on his face leaks onto my neck, dripping down the chest guard of my proofing. Teeth clenched tightly, he seethes at the mouth, pushing with all his might, pinning me closer to the ground. His eyes dilate. "You are foul! Die! Die the death you deserve!"

Rancid blood speckles my face, engulfing me in horrid stench, reminding me of the horrible animals that passed through Joachim's mouth. Insanity has taken Joachim. His eyes bear down on me. His knuckles are white as he grips his weapon. I must do something fast, or his disregard for life might be rewarded with the spilling of his own blood.

I kick out the inside of his leg, his knee drops to the floor, and I rip upward with the Bawaka, splitting the spear in half. His retaliation is swift. Using one of the broken pieces, Joachim thrusts down, over and over with the shortened shaft, using it like a stake to pierce my heart.

"You think you're the only one who knows how to do it?" screams Joachim. Grabbing my hair, he slams my head against the hard ground. Flashes of light splash across my vision. Joachim brings the stake down again and misses my heart, lodging the wood between the chest and shoulder piece. I feel his determination to push it through the armor, but no wood can penetrate the steel beneath the leather. His face wrinkles up as he stands and begins pounding on my chest like a wild beast.

Grabbing his leg, I twist it, causing him to buckle from me, landing on his side. I roll over and turn about to face him and again, he comes toward me with both shafts of the severed spear. His eyes seem to bulge from his head as he approaches, leaping back and forth with amazing speed. It is hard to tell which side he will strike from as he closes in. I throw the Bawaka to counter the approach, but he simply leaps over the spinning blade.

I block his low strike to my side, gripping his wrist and using his momentum to force his body down, but he quickly follows with an overhead strike, aimed for my neck. But I am faster. I strike the underside of his forearm with the back of mine, forcing him to release his weapon, and with a countering motion, bend at the waist, pulling his arm and send him flailing over me. I catch the Bawaka on its return trip and turn to face Joachim.

On hands and knees, Joachim stares at me like a wildcat stalking its prey, placing one hand beside the next, turning his body slightly with each step. He bares his teeth at me like an animal and I hear the faint sound of growling.

"Where is my son!" I shout in frustration.

Joachim says nothing as he moves closer.

"My son, Joachim! Where is he!" My hopes for Dorian's wellbeing are fading fast.

Joachim sinks lower to the ground.

"Damn you."

Joachim leaps.

The Bawaka leaves my hand and as it reaches Joachim, he turns enough to avoid my aiming for his neck, but not enough for his torso. The spinning blade catches the side of his stomach, tearing the stained shirt from his body, whirling his blood in all directions. Joachim falls to the ground screaming as the Bawaka comes to a halt, tangling in the soiled shirt beyond his reach and mine. I watch him clutch his steaming wound, screaming like a tortured victim.

I stand over Joachim, holding my silver stake at his neck, preventing his chance to do anything more. "What have you done with Dorian!" I say, bringing Joachim's chin up with the point of the stake. I look into his eyes; the red veins are gone.

Joachim shudders at the sight of me, as if seeing me for the first time. Scrambling, he backs against a rock, never taking his eyes off me.

"Joachim!" I say, moving closer to him.

He cries out in horror. "No—please—don't kill me!" He grabs at his arms, rubbing them, scratching them until blood spurts out. His hands go to his neck, scratching there too, scraping at his pale purplish skin. Through the wiry hair falling around his shoulders, I cannot see what torments him. Every time I reach for him, he cowers away like a helpless animal.

"I am—cold," he says.

I hear his teeth chattering; his lips, cracked and dry, tremble after every word even as he licks them. If I had water to give him, I wouldn't. He deserves to suffer.

"Joachim," I start again slowly, fearing I might set him back into hysteria. "Where is Dorian?"

This time, for some reason, the name triggers something inside him. His eyes widen in response, holding up his fingers, pointing at nothing in particular. "Dorian—Dorian is gone— they took him, Lord Wolfgang—they took him!" he whimpers. He leans forward, slipping to his knees, sobbing on the floor like a demented child.

I grab him and shake him violently. "Worm! You're lying." Moving the silver stake to his neck, I press, breaking the surface of the skin. A thin stream of blood trickles down, passing along his spidery veins. "Lie again, and it will be your last word."

"No. No! I swear it! I swear it! I do not lie!" His words are lost in the collection of spit in his mouth. Saliva seeps from both corners.

"You destroyed everything!" I say, shaking him. "You took Dorian, killed Diana, and burned my home. Why?" I shout, shaking him harder.

"No! Lord Wolfgang, please. I would never! You must believe me," he says, pleading for sanctuary. Now he is the one holding my arms. I see his composure returning. For a moment I feel he is telling the truth, but something doesn't feel right. He is not staring into my eyes, but at my neck, captivated for some reason. With every beat of my heart, my neck pulses and his eyes twitch.

Leaning forward, I grab Joachim's hair and pull it aside. The suddenness makes him flinch. Resting within the depression of his neck lie two festering puncture marks.

"You bastard," I say, standing up, raising the silver stake to his face. The blood in my body rushes to my head. I will torture him first. Then kill him.

Joachim's hand goes to his neck. "Oh God, no!" He falls forward into a fetal position, grabbing at his throat again and again, writhing on the floor as if poisoned.

I watch Joachim in disgust, wanting to drive the cold silver stake through his bleak heart. Joachim has turned and there's no doubt the same has happened for Dorian. Has it come to this? I try to shun the thought of having to kill my own son as I bring the silver stake to Joachim's forehead.

"This wasn't my doing, you must believe me, please! I would never!"

"You've destroyed everything," I say. "Everything I loved."

"You have to believe me! Please!" Joachim says, holding his hands out as if they would protect him. "They took us from Wolfgang Manor and brought us here to this wretched place. It was them. You must believe me."

I pause.

"They knew you would come here."

They?

I bring my face to meet Joachim's. "Who?" I etch a line into Joachim's face. Blood trails from the edge of his eye to the tip of his chin.

"The Carnalreesee."

The name echoes in my head like a ripple of water, remembering what Roul said before he died. There had been a man he'd seen, not a boy. And the man was with the Carnalreesee. I lower the stake to Joachim's chest, pricking it with the point. "You are one of them."

Joachim's eyes open wide. He shakes his head violently. "I'm not! I swear it." He grabs my forearms. "They abducted us, took us and separated us here. They beat us like slaves. I begged for food and they laughed. I remember one of them saying to give me water or I'll die, so the others finally agreed." Joachim's breath is fast between his words. "But when I drank the water, something was wrong. It tasted awful. Horrible and crude. It was the last thing I remember until some time ago. I woke next to the river," he says, pointing over his head.

I stare at Joachim for a moment. There is fear in his eyes. Despite his words, I never take the stake from his chest.

"From that point on, I was alone and cold, left with nothing. Dorian and the Carnalreesee were gone. Things came for me in dark. Monsters. Atrocities. I could barely defend myself. After making a weapon and finding kindling for fire, I sought food. The pains in my stomach were too much to bare. They were unlike anything I've ever felt." He clenches at his stomach. "The meat is like ash in my mouth, glass in my throat, the juices gone. The more I cook it, the worse it tastes. And the fire," Joachim turns his eyes away as if in reverie. "A never-ending cold. No matter how close I come to it, its warmth eludes me."

His symptoms are evident to me now. He is a vampire. But despite his plea for humanity, I spare him none. By choice or not, he was with the Carnalreesee and is now a part of them.

I grab him by the shoulders and lift him to his feet. The look on his face is one of sheer horror. "I'm not going to kill you."

His expression changes at the sound of my words. "Then you believe me," Joachim says, managing to stand on his own.

I pull back, twirling the stake in my hand and brace my arm across his chest to slam him against a rock, then point the stake over his heart. "I didn't say that."

He raises his arms helplessly. "Lord Wolfgang, you have to trust me."

"I have every reason not to trust you."

The day I killed his mother comes rushing back, when I fastened her to the post in the town square. I vividly recall the villagers around me chanting *Vampire, the devil's offspring. Kill the vampire,* they said, *kill her.* And there stood Joachim, just a teenage boy, watching his mother cry tears of blood as broken bottles struck her naked body. I warned him what terror he would behold, but he insisted he wanted to see the work of the famous Wolfgang, even if it was his own mother who was going to die. I should have known what would happen, should have listened to Bronin. I was bestowing charity at the time, and now I see what charity has brought me. Joachim's desire for revenge has stayed with him all this time. How long he has waited. So many years.

I feel cold hands touch my elbow and shudder from Joachim's touch. "Whatever it is you are thinking, it isn't so." Joachim's loose wiry hair falls across his face. For a moment, I remember him huddled over his dying mother. Him kissing her cheek and whispering to her he would exact retribution for her one day. Do all that he could. How similar I was, leaning over my Diana, watching her body burn away. It all makes sense. Someone he loved for someone I loved.

Anger wells inside me like a great furnace. I turn to face him, squeezing the stake tightly in my hands.

All empathy seems to have left Joachim's face. "I loved her too," he says, in a solemn tone. "More than you know."

I frown at Joachim's words. They are distant to me. There is no way of knowing what is real or not. He loved my Diana? His attempt at sympathy may be a ploy. He may be reading my thoughts. Vampires are notorious for such things.

"What do you know of love, Joachim?" I say, shaking my head. I move away from him, looking over my shoulder. "Do you know your way through these caverns?"

"Only some," Joachim says.

"That will do. You are going to help me find Dorian."

"But I do not know where the Carnalreesee have taken him."

"I know, that's why you're going to take me to the place where you last saw him."

CHAPTER
XXII

THE WAY THROUGH THE CAVERNS is cold and desolate. I follow closely behind Joachim as he navigates between rocks and over creeks. Mist dusts my face from the river as the water breaks and splashes against the walls, the water running its usual course upward. I stare at the churning liquid, remembering what it did to me, as if it had an agenda, existed purposely to twist my mind into clay. And how it morphed my thoughts. To have another episode like that would destroy me, end my search for Dorian and allow Joachim to go free.

Shifting my eyes back on Joachim, I notice his pace quickens and I find myself hastening my own movement. He seems to have a renewed interest in finding Dorian and I can't help to wonder about the reason why. Maybe it's because he knows I'll drive my blade into his skull or maybe, he still really cares for Dorian. I have seen cases before where victims of the curse were able to suppress the urges of vampirism and remember their human side. Regardless of what was retained, regardless of what was confessed or absolved, they would die in the end. There is no place for vampires in this world, good or bad, and they will die by my hand. With or without God on my side.

Joachim's clothes are soiled a muddy brown. Splashing through far stretches of shallow water, it is no surprise that I too become the same color. Some areas near the river's bank are mud traps and not once, but twice, I find myself falling behind, slowing down because of the muck. He leads on without stopping, never looking back to see if I follow. He is determined.

"Joachim. Slow down."

He doesn't answer. "Joachim!" It's too late and I lose sight of him.

Pulling my leg from the mud, I shout. "Joachim!" Still no answer.

From one rock to another, I take short leaps, peering between boulders and broken pieces of wood. My eyes scan dark crevices revealing dancing shadows from torchlight. Joachim knew. He was prepared. Going this way would hinder me, slow me down.

"Joachim!" I call out again, my anxiety rising. A cool breeze blows across my face as I pass between two stones. There is Joachim in the distance, walking a sweeping expanse of flat ground. Wind generated from the river pushes my body forward as it whips my hair about my shoulders. Joachim is in his own world, walking slowly in a straight line. He does not hear me. His head moves back and forth, watching the ground, studying it. As I move out into the open, I get this sudden feeling of exposure. My hand is ready to throw the Bawaka in an instant, yet there is no foe to combat, no new horror to encounter. Only Joachim, who stands solemnly at the center of an open plain, his crushed velvet tunic rippling from the gusts.

I come up behind him before he has a chance to flee. "Do that again—"

"It was here," he says, cutting my speech off. "Here is where they beat us." Joachim points to dark-colored areas on the ground, maybe once red, now brown. "It was here they made me drink the water. It was the last time I saw Dorian."

When I look about the vast openness of the area, I see nothing particular about it that would warrant it striking. There are a few scattered boulders and old animal bones. Not even spiderwebs linger about. There is nothing here to go on as I circle around, passing by the river edge, searching near an outlying crop of stacked rubble. As I head back to Joachim, I notice he is close to the ground, crouching. Before I question his motive, he runs his fingers along one of the dark spots. What's he doing now?

His hand goes to his mouth and there is no time for me to react. His head turns to me with eyes red, baring fangs of a yellowish brown. Readying my blade, I realize I will have to find Dorian on my own after all.

But Joachim doesn't attack. His composure restrains him, as if fighting some internal battle.

"If you want to find your son, this is the only way," Joachim says. His voice is changed, possessed by something other than himself. Before I can say a word, he takes off, darting among the rocks in the direction we have not yet traversed.

I have no choice but to follow. His speed is incredible, not like before when we fought. It's the frenzy. The blood. His senses are developing fast. It's only a matter of time before he is lost to the curse and I drive my stake through his heart.

Chasing after him, I wonder at the ethics I'm practicing. Following a vampire into a darkness to search for a son who is most likely dead. I feel like the devil is guiding me deeper into his domain, and I am gladly following him into that hellish realm. What does it matter at this point? Having lost everything, nothing matters anymore, especially my own safety.

Climbing the rocks proves difficult for me as Joachim dashes about them like a beast in the forest. Despite the pain in my shoulder and the scars on my face, the cold air gives me comfort as I ascend. Rock after rock, I pull myself along, feeling the ache and burn of my rib, but determination keeps me going.

Reaching the top, a vast darkness stretches before me, and within in it, a faint spattering of light decorates the blackness in splotches. Are they torches? I hear the roar of the river nearby and the faint mist of the water reminds me of the strange things that happened to me days ago. Has it been that long? It's impossible to tell time passing in the dark.

Joachim says nothing as I follow him. It is the blind leading the blind, but how much of Joachim's unknowing is really true. We pass the torches I saw only moments ago and realize they mark a path. Joachim sniffs the air and continues forward, moving past the carcasses of eviscerated animals. As he presses on, the more I realize we are in the den of some creature. The ground continues on a descending slope and the pressure in my ears hurts.

"This way," Joachim says solemnly in the same tone he always used when serving my family.

Faster and faster he moves, and I find myself running to keep up. The scent must be stronger. The blood of my son. I feel like a hunter with his hound, tracking the wounded to its resting place where he would claim his reward without a fight. I have a feeling what I will find may terrify me.

The howling we can hear in the distance has no effect on Joachim. He keeps going, passing his gaze back and forth as he comes to large openings in the cavern walls, long tunnels that split at various intersections. I feel I'm racing against time with Joachim so determined to find Dorian. I follow him down a wet cave full of thick fog, and progression slows due to the inability to see.

"Joachim!" I say, hoping he doesn't go too far without me, but it's too late to worry. I no longer see him and the torches in the walls provide minimal light. It will be easy to get lost in the maze of tunnels.

"Joachim!" I shout a second time. The only reply is my echo. The howling is closer and I hear the pattering of nails on stone. Pressing my body against the cave wall, I start making my way forward with as little noise as possible. I am certain the daver hounds are near and not few in number.

Moving inside a tunnel system far underground is nerve-racking. The endless roar of the river sounds like a beast in perpetual torment. It's enough to drown out the noise I make. Soon the wall gives way to an opening that expands in the distance and ends abruptly. Coming to a halt before an opening of what seems to be the side of a cliff, a sharp ledge bears down from my feet. Off to the side, the rushing water of the Faust River gushes from an immense opening in the side of the rock. With no solid rock bed to carry its normal ascension, it pummels down into the massive void below, vanishing into darkness. Did its source of power end here, or was it following the natural contour of the riverbed?

I turn around to go back the way I came and stop.

Daver hounds are waiting for me. Twelve of them. More than double from the encounter in the dungeons. Teeth set in overexposed gums—blood and bile drip from their jaws as if they've recently finished a meal. Some of them lick their teeth, their serpentine tongues thin at the ends. There are a few with their ribs exposed from the inside, their guts hanging out as if they'd been attacked by something. I wonder if Joachim had anything to do with it. One of them gives a ghastly howl and they all shift.

Snarling their teeth, they come for me, running at full speed. Between the roar of the waterfall and their growling, the clattering of their claws is lost and I counter. Pulling the Bawaka and the silver stake from my belt, I twist and wield my weapons with deadly precision. Immediately I sever the throat of one daver hound as I ram the stake through the belly of another, coming underneath it as it leaps for me, ensnaring my weapon. More attack me at the same time, yet I can't address them all. Some clamp onto my legs, two grapple with my arms. If they wrestle me to the ground, all will be lost.

With all my strength I rip the silver stake free from the dead daver hound's stomach, and drive it through the brains of the two clamped to my arm. With a flick of my wrist, I spin the blade in an arc, cutting the leg off one and slashing the face of another. Their barks wither into yelps as they cower from me, hobbling away, ears flat against their wrinkled heads.

They form a circle around me, taking steps back and forth, snapping their teeth, flaring their nostrils. One comes too close and I drive the stake through the top of its head, sending it into spasms as blood gurgles from its mouth.

"Is that it?" I shout to the hounds. "Who sent you?"

I know they won't answer me, but my frustration peaks. With Joachim gone, how will I find Dorian? I swipe my blade at another daver hound and it jumps back with a growl. The fog is getting thicker and more hounds arrive. Soon, I can't see anything.

I twirl the torch around me to keep the hounds at bay, taking steps backwards so that my backside is protected by the wall. Their growls continue as the back of my heels hit stone. Inching toward the way I started, I hear the clicking of the daver hounds' feet and the breathing of their hanging tongues. Then the growling increases and I imagine their breath pushing the smoke in and out of their lungs. Louder it continues and I know it's only a matter of time. I keep inching along the wall.

There is a sudden upset of yelping and roars as chaos unfolds in the blinding fog. There is swirling mist and the sound of sticks breaking. Yelps turn into growls and soon it sounds like there are hundreds of daver hounds fighting over a piece of meat. The commotion causes the fog to dissipate and through it I see the grey skin of the daver hounds moving around in a frenzy, lashing with their teeth at something. An animal perhaps? Suddenly hands appear through the mist and snap the neck of a daver hound. More crunching. More breaking. Hands lash out again, turning the daver hounds' skin red with its long nails. High pitch screams come from the hounds' torment and I know what is in there will come for me next.

I make to move, but something has my leg. I burn the side of the daver hound with my torch and it releases, scurrying away with skin ablaze. Through the clearing fog, more hounds are running to me, mouths open, tongues dripping. In a sudden moment, something lands on top of them like a hellish demon, lashing out with its long nails, and wiry hair bouncing about its shoulders. With both hands it braces their heads against the ground with pressure, pushing and crushing the fluids from their eye sockets. Through its dirty hair, I see fangs and they rip into the side of the daver hound's neck.

Its red eyes look up at me. Joachim.

How different he looks. The shirt he was wearing is gone. His pants are nearly torn away. All that remains are the boots on his feet. I stare at him as he feasts on the beasts, sucking their blood. His pupils dilate as his mouth releases. He sucks in a deep breath.

"You need to get out of here," he says, wiping blood away from his mouth. "More are coming."

Another daver hound bites into Joachim's shoulder from behind. Joachim screams and grabs the back of the beast's neck, pulling it free, ripping his own pale skin in the process. Blood gushes from his neck but it seems not to affect him. In fact, he is smiling. Joachim tears its neck out and the beast falls limp.

"Go!"

I take off as dozens of daver hounds come pouring in, clamoring over Joachim like a river of canines. I hear him yelling at the hounds, distracting them as I exit the tunnel. I do not know where to go. There are so many different ways, so many openings.

I need to keep moving. Howling and barking come from some of the passages so I run in the opposite direction, descending further into the cave system. Crossing over bridges and leaping off stones, I realize the sound is still following me. I look over my shoulder to find more daver hounds chasing after me, Joachim at the lead, slamming the dogs into the walls and tossing them into the air. He is still trying to protect me. Even though they are attacking him, they are moving past him as well. It's not his blood they want; it's mine.

I keep running. There is a crash somewhere above me and boulders come tumbling down. Another collapse? More barking from another direction makes me realize the tunnels are more than just passageways. They are the homes to these devilish creatures. More join the pack and they are closing on me. Joachim is still there, biting and beating them into bloody pulps. The tide won't turn with these impossible odds.

There is a flash of light and suddenly I'm back in the room with my beloved Diana when we were young, back in her father's house, in her bedroom. It is raining outside and I am soaked to the bone. What is happening to me? Am I dreaming again?

No. Not now. Now is not the time, Diana!

I watch myself undress and climb into that warm bed with her. So soft, those plush pillows.

Stop! What are you doing?

I find myself yelling at myself. I must be going insane. There is a rap at the door to her room. Quick Tenor! It's my father. He's going to kill you! You need to get out! I fall out of the bed and onto the floor.

Splashing into a small creek that has escaped the main part of the river, I stand in the shallow water gasping for air. There is brilliant white light all around me, and just as I come to, it vanishes, leaving me in the dark tunnel with only the torch lit in my hand. I try to get a grip on reality. What is wrong with me?

More barking from daver hounds. More shouting from Joachim. I stand up and start running through the dark corridor again

"Tenor!" comes a voice further up the passage. No. Not again. I want to ignore the voice, but I'm running in the direction of it with nowhere else to go.

"Tenor!" comes the voice again.

I know that voice.

From the darkness, Father Bronin emerges. He holds a brilliant torch over his head and in the other hand, one of his holy flasks. "God's will, you're alive!"

I am relieved to all ends. My friend. There is so much I want to ask him, but my breath prevents me from speaking. Hands on my knees, I hear the echoing bark of the daver hounds coming.

"Come, Tenor, there is no time," Bronin says. His blue eyes are bright and alert.

"Wait," I say, grabbing his arm. "I found him."

"Found who?"

Without looking back, I feel Joachim's presence approaching. The familiar power he holds. That of the vampire I have hunted for so long.

I turn to meet him, to thank him for what he's done, but something isn't right.

His face is screwed up and his eyes are wide. "You!" says Joachim; it is the last word he says as glass shatters against him and his skin bursts into flames.

"No!" I cry out.

Joachim screams as he staggers and crumples to the floor, rolling around in agony.

Jumping away to avoid the fire, I look to Bronin, grasping the cloth at his chest, and shaking him violently. "Why!"

There is a look of horror and confusion on Bronin's face as he tries to stammer out the words. "He was one of them. A Carnalreesee."

I back away from Bronin speechless and turn to look at the smoldering ruin of Joachim's remains. Crouching, I hold my hands out before the dying embers of his body, watching the last chance I have at finding Dorian go with them. "Rrraahhhh!" I shout in frustration. "Dammit!"

"Tenor, please," says Bronin, grabbing my shoulder. "Snap out of it."

I push Bronin back. "Stay away from me."

"We cannot stay." There is genuine concern in his eyes.

The daver hounds howl in the distance. I can't help but look at the ashes of Joachim's body.

"Not all is lost," says Bronin.

I turn to face him. "Yes, it is. I have failed."

"Don't be so sure of that," says Bronin. "I know where they've taken Dorian."

CHAPTER XXIII

OVER AND OVER, THE LOOK of horror on Joachim's face clouds my head. That stare of distaste, hatred, and fear; all of them in one expression, burning in the holy fire of God. Condemned to hell. Now I follow the man who sentenced him to death. Bronin gave no warning. No trial.

There wasn't a chance to explain. No action to take. It all happened so fast.

"He was one of them," says Bronin as we pass through a dark passageway. His pace is quick, yet not as quick as Joachim's was. "Since the time you killed his mother and took him in. What did you expect, Tenor? The devil. The Carnalreesee. He aligned himself with them. I never trusted the man the day you welcomed him in your home. Told you not to harbor the children of the parents you slay. They are broken, my son. It never changes."

The notion has crossed my mind before. There were times I questioned the loyalty from Joachim, no doubt. But Bronin didn't see what I had seen, the circumstance of things. Joachim saved my life, yet shuddered from the sight of Bronin. My mind lingers for some time, not knowing what really happened. But I soon realize, does it really matter? I will never know.

"Hurry. We must keep moving. If my assumption is correct, there isn't much time."

My mind races. Assumption? What exactly did Bronin know? I say nothing despite my desire to know. I have known the man since I was a child. He saved my life more than once, and possessed all the wisdom of God within him like an earthbound saint. I give him the benefit of the doubt. The man is old and run down. This place has claimed more of his soul than he probably knows and I am sure he thinks the same for me. I trust him, for I have nothing left to believe in. He is more than a man of God to me. He is a friend, the only one I have left it seems.

Running through another corridor, I follow Bronin closely, noticing his muscles tense through the various tears in his black garb. I know his adrenaline is peaking. After crossing a chasm and severing the ropes to the bridge, the daver hounds' pursuit ends. They watch us from afar, jumping over one another, barking and whining as we make our escape.

I notice a long cut on Bronin's forehead I did not see before. He must have gone through hell at the time of our separation. The library transformed to a fiery inferno. The burning debris falling down like rain. Yet all this time he was alive. He must have traversed other paths, seen events I did not. How he found me, I do not know. I know if I ask him, his answer will be God.

"Down there," says Bronin.

We are at the crest of a long flight of descending stairs. Each step I take, the stones seem to tremble from the pressure.

"If you linger too long, they will break." I have not taken but ten steps before stopping at a gaping hole. I hear creaking and know I must press forward. Leaping across with ease, I turn back to help catch Bronin as he clears the gap. Rocks skitter across the steps, falling off the edge, descending into a void of air. Moving along more cracked surfaces, we eventually reach the bottom and come to understand the magnitude of the chamber. Tall pillars of stone reach to the ceiling and line the walkway directly in the center pathway. To its sides, great burning urns light the entire cave. In either direction, jagged rocks form a natural barrier around the walkway. It would be impossible to traverse its hidden secrets. Great swooping tunnels enter and exit at different levels, some hundreds of feet in the air, some below eye level. Its grandness swallows me up. Bronin pushes past me, pointing at the far end of the walkway.

"That is where the Carnalreesee took Dorian. Beyond the doors." I hear him breathing heavily. "Come. Time is precious," he says without stopping. Clearly, he is on a mission. The doors are massive and remain open wide, welcoming anyone to come in. Bronin doesn't wait for me and already is halfway across the walkway when I realize how quiet the surroundings are. There are no sounds from the river in the distance, no echoes from scattering rocks as we pass. Nothing. Only the scraping of our boots across stone.

"I had counted six Carnalreesee," Bronin says over his shoulder, never taking a break in his stride. Following behind him, I contemplate his words. "Six Carnalreesee escorting Dorian by the wrists." Bronin continues on about the vampires as if they have some significant meaning. It is clear they have my son. "Six," he says again, then stops in mid-stride. "That's not good," he whispers over his shoulder to me.

I give him a puzzling look. His eyes go wide. "There's supposed to be seven." In the distance, a thunderous roar echoes through the cavern like an explosion. It's followed by the sound of crumbling rocks and falling stalactites until the avalanche ceases completely. I look to Bronin for answers. He shrugs his shoulders and I look back into the vastness of the cave. All is quiet again, except for the faintest sound of squeaking. It gets louder and louder, turning into hideous shrieks, forcing me to cover my ears.

"Get back!" shouts Bronin. I scramble, taking cover behind one of the blazing urns. Sitting with my back against it, I turn my head to see Bronin doing the same. He peers his head around the side, ducking it back in. Bats swarm past, flying with incredible speed. One after another, their wings flap in a frenzy. Another moment and they would have taken our heads off. A bat flops to the ground near my leg, apparently having hit the urn in its flight. Bouncing around like a fish out of water. I bring my boot down on it, crushing its body over the stone floor.

I look over at Bronin to make sure he is all right and he is staring off into nothing. His eyes look glazed over as if in a trance.

High above, the bats swarm about in synchronized fashion, shrieking louder and never ceasing. They vanish through the open doorway, the passage Bronin and I intend to go through.

"Quick!" I say, leaping up. Bronin seems to snap out of his trance, startled at my sudden outburst. Running over to him, I grab him by the shirt, forcing him to get up. "You said six Carnalreesee," I say, looking into his icy blue eyes. "That was the seventh!" Only the strongest of vampires have the ability to change into a swarm of bats. In most cases, it is their preferred method of movement when traveling alone. If the Carnalreesee were of Egleaseon's chosen few, there is no doubt they possess immense power, the ability to change form. "They know we're here."

Running through the open doors, I stop before a railing, old and broken. It crumbles as my hands grip it. I am in what seems to be a circular tower chamber, a large vast open area descending down into torchlight. Stone stairs run down the course of its curved wall as far as the light will allow me to see. Hanging from the ceiling, a large mechanism with multiple cogs lies dormant in dust and cobwebs; the metal gears have a film of rust on their surface. Drooping loosely from its center are two thick chains, also red with decay. At my feet, the bones of skeletons scatter from my movement. A skull rolls along the floor and comes to a halt. There are still some bats flapping about, discontent with our presence.

A strange sound floats up from the lower levels. Music-like at first but I realize it's not music. It's chanting. Eerily it echoes up the cavity of the tower, filling the space with dread.

"I am getting *that* feeling," Bronin says suddenly. There is no need for me to ask him about it. When a priest has a "feeling" it never amounts to anything good. I look down the wide tower opening again and take a deep breath. The air tastes stale and metallic as if no surface air ever breached down here. Mixed with the voices below, I am doused with the feeling of doom.

I begin my descent; Bronin following closely behind. I wonder at the place we are at, the circumstance we are in. Skulls line the walls as we pass. They never seem to take their eyes off of me. I have seen them before—Albestan Church.

"Bronin, what is this place?" I ask, descending each step methodically.

"The Underground Monastery," he says almost simultaneously, as if anticipating my question. He is very close behind me. His words are in my ear. It takes me a moment to understand what he is saying. "Lord Egleaseon's abode. His resting place during the hours of the sun."

I increase my pace, moving as fast as I can down the stairs without tripping over myself. The Carnalreesee have brought my son to this place and I cannot imagine what for. The fear I had before was nothing compared to this. I begin running down the stairs at this point, no longer caring if I fall. At least I will get to the bottom faster. I descend into twinkling torchlight of this horrible place. It seems to take forever to reach the bottom of this pit, and when I finally do, it is destroyed beyond comprehension. Wood and rubble cover every inch of the floor making it harder to traverse its mess. The chains hanging from the center are connected to a metal and wood-framed crate, a contraption used for elevating things. Covered in webs, silvery spiders shimmer in the light as they emerge from the various shadows about the chamber.

The doors I need to pass through are across the room, open just enough where the bats escaped through. I begin climbing over the debris, scrambling toward them, tossing broken planks of wood aside. Dammit. The chanting is getting louder.

There is a loud bang from somewhere above that echoes down the tower shaft, rattling everything around me.

"Someone is coming!" says Bronin. His voice is frantic. He is having difficulty moving through the wreckage as well. I imagine the seventh member of the Carnalreesee emerging from the shadows, swooping down the stairs with long sharp nails, coming to slit our throats. I turn and focus on getting through the mayhem despite the turmoil around me. My heart is racing. Sweat drenches my face despite my cold breath.

Reaching the doors, I wedge them open enough so that my proofing can fit through. And I stop, unable to think, move, or speak. My blood runs colder than ice for I hear the worst thing a father can hear while alive on this earth—The sound of his child screaming for his life.

CHAPTER
XXIV

"NO!" I SCREAM, CHARGING FORWARD from the doors into what seems like a stadium of some sort. Arms enclose around me as Bronin uses his body weight to bring me down. Hitting the ground together, we stop abruptly against a stone wall. The wind is knocked from my lungs. Unable to speak, I look at Bronin. He seems shocked at his own actions. Using his body to hold me down, he bends close to my ear.

"What are you doing? They will kill us if we charge in on them." Anger rips me up from the inside. I want to kick Bronin off me but I can't. The chanting is louder than before.

Dorian screams again. They are torturing him.

"Get off me!" I say through clenched teeth. Bronin loosens his grip and backs away, his eyes wrought with fear. Pulling myself up, I peer over the top of the wall, just enough to conceal myself. And wish I never did.

Six figures dressed in blood red robes and golden masks surround my son. Dorian lies on his back, struggling against the ropes holding him down. A robed figure for each appendage, they pull hard on his arms and legs, stretching him across a stone table like a butcher purging his meat of blood. Across his chest, a fifth figure uses white-gloved hands to keep Dorian from further resistance. The sixth moves away from one of Dorian's hand, leaving it bloody and twitching, and proceeds to the next, carrying a hammer and a fist full of iron spikes.

"Please—don't!" begs Dorian.

I see his head moving side to side, his golden hair matted down from sweat or blood. The figure continues, ignoring him.

What is this? Red robes, white gloves. Golden masks bearing the image of tragic smiles, curved stag horns protruding from the crests. There is a sharp pain in my side and my body suddenly goes weak. Slumping against the wall is all I can do to keep myself standing. I look down at the blood. So much of it. Knife stuck in my side, a vial in its handle slowly begins filling with blood.

Bronin stares at me, pushing the knife further in. "Blood of the father," he says. A look of terror mixed with excitement is written on his face. I want to speak, but I can't. Something paralyzes my speech. He is my friend. Servant of God. I turn my head to see Dorian. A spike is driven through his other hand. The sound of iron on stone is deafening. Dorian screams. My son. My poor son. My mind is going numb. Seven Carnalreesee. I look at Bronin. All emotion is gone.

"I know what you are thinking," he says calmly. "Why am I doing this?" He grabs a hold of my face. The scent of blood is in the air. My blood. "Simple, really, to ensure the freshest blood is delivered right to us. Blood from the one who killed Egleaseon. Fused with the blood of your son, he will make the perfect vessel for our lord's return."

The contraption continues to drain blood from me. My knees waver as I lean my weight onto Bronin, the weakness almost overcoming me.

"Forgive me, Tenor, but life eternal in this world is far more obtainable." The sleeve of his robe reveals a tattoo on his wrist: an x with a line through the center. "You were right. God has forsaken everyone."

I hear the driving of another nail, the crunching of bone, Dorian's cry for mercy.

"The Carnalreesee won't give him mercy," says Bronin. "They will bleed just enough blood from his body."

It is hard for me to breathe. The knife wound is just below my bottom rib.

"Now watch what we do to your son."

Bronin grabs me by the elbows and lifts me onto the wall to further support my body. Removing the vial from the knife, he holds it up to the light, admiring it like a prized jewel.

"Blood of the father," he says, smiling.

A bolt bursts out the backside of Bronin's hand, sending the vial soaring through the air. Screaming, he grabs his hand as I watch the tiny glass bottle bounce off a rock and shatter across the floor.

"You bastard!" yells Bronin, clutching his bloody hand. I watch him turn toward the darkness behind us, teeth clenched, growling and screaming. Another bolt flies at him but he drops to the floor, rolling toward the stairs. With one quick movement, he is back on his feet, fleeing down the stairs. Left alone, I watch my life's blood dripping onto the floor. Somehow I clutch the dagger and begin to retract it. I feel the edge of it catching the side of my rib. The pain is unbearable. I can't pull it out all the way. I lean on the wall, sliding to the floor, my back against stone, my vision wavering in and out, struggling with the knife. There is something moving toward me. A figure? A monster? What does it matter? Death will come soon.

There is pressure at my side. In one swift motion, the knife is pulled from my body. There is a clatter of metal on the floor. Bandages are shoved into my wound, turning them red. And then comes a voice I thought I would never hear again.

"You seem to be in a sad state of affairs, Lord Wolfgang."

"Kronklich," I manage to say.

"Yes, it's me. In the flesh."

"How did you—you're here."

"'Course I am. Can't have you dying on me. Not yet."

Am I delirious, hearing Kronklich's voice, envisioning him before me? He seems real enough. Thoughts about the carriage crashing and Manson rush to me. "How did you—"

"Now's not the time," he says, helping me sit up. "We have to save your son. Here, chew this." He puts something in my mouth and it begins tingling my tongue. The cold juices race down my throat.

Loading a bolt onto his crossbow, I notice Kronklich's recent handiwork. He's fashioned his cane to the foregrip and barrel as an easier way to retract the blade. Top hat gone, his grey suit is still moderately intact, but torn in places with a large gash across the back, exposing the white linen underneath. "Here they come," he says, spinning around and firing a shot.

Energy is returning to me. Whatever Kronklich gave me is reacting fast. It runs through my body, bringing life back to my joints and muscles. Blood surges through my veins invigorating me with new hope. I roll to my side and see Kronklich running down the stairs toward Dorian and the Carnalreesee. He won't survive without my help.

With newfound strength, I collect myself from the ground and stagger down the stairs. My heart is racing. "Dorian!" I shout, taking two steps for every one of Kronklich's. There is no response from him. His hands and feet bound and nailed, he has been crucified to the slab. "Kronklich!" I shout, and he immediately crouches to one knee, loading his crossbow. The Bawaka leaves my hand with furious speed, over Kronklich's head, straight toward our assailants.

The Carnalreesee spread like frenzied ants; their vampire speed convoluting their positions, making it impossible to hit any target. Leaping over Kronklich's head, I land rolling onto the floor, catching the return trip of the Bawaka. Just when a Carnalreesee appears next to me, it vanishes instantly as Kronklich's bolt passes by.

Giant burning urns light the entire area of the ritual floor. Against the far wall, large stone pillars support the upper portions of a mausoleum. It is there I see Dorian sprawled across the stone slab, blood seeping from his body. Bronin is somewhere near, but I've lost sight of him. The bastard.

One of the Carnalreesee suddenly stops next to an urn, his golden mask glinting in the firelight. "Bronin, where is his blood?" it shouts from under that hideous mask. "You promised us his blood!"

"It's there in front of you!" he says, pointing at me from behind one of the pillars. I cannot see what he is doing.

"You're pathetic," says the Carnalreesee as it comes for me, dagger in hand, faster than I can anticipate. All I can do is deflect its assault as it slashes and stabs at me, the whole while the mask never moving from its locked position. Such strength. Such precision. They must come from a strong lineage of vampires.

Spinning my Bawaka as fast as I can, I move it across my body like a shield as the Carnalreesee drives its dagger at my chest. Caught in a whirlwind fury, the dagger flies from its hand, the ringing sound of metal on metal lingers until the dagger bangs and clatters along the floor. I lash out, slicing forward, but the Carnalreesee is too fast. It leaps into the air over my head and is gone from my sight. From the corner of my eye, I see Kronklich firing a bolt at a different Carnalreesee but it simply ricochets off one of the urns.

"Behind you!" warns Kronklich.

I feel the air move over my head as I duck from an attack. Instantly I am tackled in the gut, the cold mask of the Carnalreesee pushing hard into my side, right over the wound where Bronin stabbed me. The Carnalreesee and I go down, rolling over one another, knocking into a fire urn, spilling its contents of boiling oil over the floor. The heat is unbearable against the scars on my face, reminding me again what I've been through these past few days.

Struggling with each other's arms, the Carnalreesee stares at me through the hollow eyes of the mask, attempting to pin my head to the ground. My eyes level with the oil and watch it slowly spread its way toward me. I take a deep breath and push against the vampire, but its strength is far superior to mine. I try one more approach, changing the pressure of one arm to the next, forcing its hand down in the burning liquid.

The reaction is instant. Burning through the white glove, the Carnalreesee screeches as it flings itself off me. I roll away before the oil burns me too. Kronklich is fighting one of them near a pillar. Slashing at Kronklich with its long nails, the Carnalreesee is unable to rip him open due to the barrier. I throw the Bawaka at him, but the bastard tucks forward, dodging my attack with ease. The return trip isn't anticipated and as he continues to flail at Kronklich, the blades hit the side of the golden mask, cracking the bottom portion of the mouth, exposing the yellow fangs of a vampire underneath. Kronklich leaps back, twirls his unloaded crossbow like a baton and retracts his cane sword from the underside of the barrel, slashing through the robes of his assailant. Red cloth scatters as the two of them keep at it. Something runs into the back of me and I am sent sprawling forward into the arms of two Carnalreesee, their nails digging into my flesh through their white gloves. Held up like a prisoner, one of the three Carnalreesee comes faster than I can react and drives its hand into the wound in my side. My vision blacks out suddenly from the pain and I slump in their arms. There are strikes to my chest where the proofing holds a majority of the steel to protect my vital organs. Over and over, the Carnalreesee beat me, forcing blood out of my mouth.

"Kronklich, don't—" is all I manage to say as Kronklich comes from behind, driving his cane sword through the back of the one delivering the blows. At first, the Carnalreesee seems stunned, but recovers instantly, swooping its arm and back-handing Kronklich's chest, sending him clean through a stone pillar. Immediately, the integrity of the mausoleum responds, breaking away from part of its roof and smashing onto the floor. The impact is startling, shaking the earth beneath and knocking everyone to the ground.

Before there is a chance for me to retaliate, the Carnalreesee dart away. I let loose my Bawaka and it spins away in a frenzy, making contact with one of them, only to be batted away like a toy. Blended from a mixture of silver and steel; I am at a loss to find it useless. A blade folded more than three hundred times; how can it be? My weapon has destroyed countless vampires. Maybe its sacred power has vanished along with my faith.

My attention goes to Kronklich lying in a pile of stone and dust. He isn't moving. "Kronklich!" I yell. There is no response. As I make my way to him, one of the fire urns tips over, gushing forth its burning liquid, separating me from him.

A loud voice calls out over cracking walls and roaring flames. "So this is what it's come down to," Bronin says, emerging from behind the smoldering urn. The dagger used to stab me is in his hand, and in the other, a flask of holy fire. Through the blazing embers of red and orange, Bronin's blue eyes glare at me with a desire I've never seen before. A hunger for power and I am his gateway to immortality; the blood in my veins is the key to it all. I watch him step away from the urn, never taking his eyes off me.

"You cannot comprehend the trouble it took me to get you here," he says, hopping down from one stone to the next. He points the knife at me. "I *will* have your blood." Anticipating his next move, I dart forward but instantly I'm thwarted. His flask misses my face, exploding on the ground near my boots. Jumping back, I am trapped in a ring of fire. Bronin jumps down into the circle with me and there is nowhere to go. We begin circling each other and I cannot tell what he will do next. Another flask in his hand could destroy us both.

"A little assurance you will cooperate," Bronin says, shaking the flask with his fingers.

My hand instinctively passes over the Bawaka; my fingers caress the grooves of the leathered cross handle.

"Seems you have a death wish," says Bronin. "Have you strayed so far from God, Tenor? One as obedient as you. Even your one redeeming quality has seemed to elude you."

Bronin's words are convoluting. It is hard for me to concentrate. My thoughts are still overcome by the betrayal and the lies. I see Kronklich stirring from the corner of my eye but I dare not look.

"Father!" comes a voice, so dearly missed I've almost forgotten what it sounds like. I turn my head to see Dorian carried from the stone altar over one of the Carnalreesee's shoulder. He reaches out his hands toward me.

"Dorian!" I cry out.

Bronin leaps for me, knife aimed at my throat. Distracted only for a second, I wait for the knife to plunge past my proofing and serrate my flesh. Instead, Bronin is sent crumpling to the ground. With a bolt stuck in his leg and blood gushing profusely, he clutches at it screaming in agony. I see Kronklich leaning against a rock, crossbow in hand.

A loud cracking sound issues forward and the ground buckles at the broken column near the mausoleum. With the support of the chamber dwindling, other columns begin snapping at their foundations, stone turning in on itself, exploding in multiple directions. A massive void opens in the ground, swallowing everything in its path. Trapped between burning oil and crumbling earth, there is little room for escape. I manage to see the golden locks of Dorian's hair one last time before sliding down into the dark hole that consumes everything around me. *My son. I am sorry. I have failed you and your mother. I remember what she said to me when I saw her last. I had to save you, Dorian. It was my intent from the beginning. I swear it.* Darkness is closing around me. I remember the day before all this madness began, watching Dorian and Diana in the courtyard, my sun and moon, and I as the earth, watching from the window. *Together. So loving, so innocent.* With the moon losing orbit, and the sun fading, the earth becomes a distant memory.

Rock and dirt suffocate me as I am swallowed in the avalanche, fire from the burning oil splashing all around me. In a matter of seconds, I am delivered to the depths of hell where I know judgment awaits me. My new life in eternal damnation.

CHAPTER
XXV

Suffocation. I dare not open my mouth or the dirt will flow in. I cannot feel my arms or legs, yet I feel something squirming against my face. Anxiety sets in. Am I alive? I experience the feeling where one holds one's breath and one's heartbeat increases. Oxygen is running out, its nourishing qualities fading.

Somewhere inside—somewhere deep—my desire to live lingers. Whether it belongs to me or not, it does not matter. I need to be free. Something is coming, an angel or demon, but my hand breaks through. I exhume myself from broken rocks and pebbles. Flakes of dirt tickle my lungs as I gasp, choking uncontrollably. There is someone else coughing too. I want to open my eyes but they burn from heat and smoke. Fire. I know it is all around me. God has judged me, sending me down instead of up, purging the world of sinners and bad fathers. I am left to fend on my own among the suffering and tormented, the wicked and the damned.

With forearms and elbows, I drag my body from the dirt, relieved from the relentless force of gravity. Fighting against the sting of opening my eyes, I am able to discern nothing. Everything is a blur. I cannot stand. The ceiling is low. Inching along, desperately I make my way forward, the only direction I can go. To my sides and behind is the unforgiving fire. The sound of coughing becomes louder as I continue, struggling toward something—anything but here.

Like a snake slithering from its hole, I exit into a larger space, disoriented, confused. Through a fit of coughing, I hear my name called. Could it be?

"Kronklich." I struggle between breaths. "Kronklich." The fading smoke reveals a grey-suited figure, disheveled and bruised, staggering through the glow of orange flame. Like an angel sent to rescue me, there is comfort in seeing Kronklich.

"You're not dead."

Kronklich manages a smile. "That's the second time today you've said that."

I want to laugh but it hurts. I am weak at the knees and Kronklich uses his cane to balance himself.

Words cannot express how glad I am to have him down here with me. These past days of solitude have chipped away my soul. I do not know who I am anymore. Seems I have lost everything, including my own life. Dorian is gone and the Carnalreesee have him. The church I once served is nothing more than a conspiracy. All this time and I never knew of its corruption. It makes me wonder how far its roots went, or if Nestor was one of them, or even the Archbishop himself. How would I know? Who could tell? I try to shun the thought of the blanket over my eyes, but it seems my whole existence has been meaningless. My purpose in life—meaningless!

Kronklich stares at me, waiting to hear my next plan of action. The look on his face is grave and I know he is thinking what I am thinking. There is no way out of here. Everything has collapsed on itself. Egleaseon's ruin is our tomb.

Awkward silence lingers for a moment. There is the faint sound of breath and I look around, knowing it is not Kronklich's.

"What is that?" I ask, moving past him, away from the glowing light of dying flames and closer to the foreboding darkness around us. The breathing is watery and disturbed with wretched coughing. Within the shadows, I make out the faint outline of a figure. A man impaled on a stalagmite. It is Bronin.

His body convulses with each attempt at movement. I try to make sense of the impossible angles his limbs, contorted and bloody, are positioned in. Legs and arms bent back and broken. Bronin reaches for the large stone spike protruding from his abdomen, but his fingertips, wet with blood, keep slipping off the glistening surface. Twitching like a web-snared fly, his head snaps toward to me. Blood oozes from his mouth. His speech is watery.

"Please," Bronin begs, but his words are lost in the gurgling of blood.

I stand before him, watching his form tremble, coughing blood. I have no words for Bronin. The man has destroyed everything I ever loved. His eyes were once a brilliant blue, but now they are pale, the fierce gaze gone. Fear changes a man. Bronin tries to speak again but there is too much blood. He will drown in it.

Good.

I feel a hand on my shoulder. I'm not sure how long Kronklich has been watching me, but I am grateful for his company. I have no idea what to do now. The one person I thought was my friend will die, the Carnalreesee took my son, and I am trapped in this godforsaken place. This is my punishment for falling away from faith.

How could I not? Where has God been in all this? Villages attacked by monsters, churches corrupted by monsters, children kidnapped by monsters. These thoughts plague my mind and I am sickened. I need to do something, but what?

There is a faint glow beyond Bronin's body and I stop. The hairs on my neck rise. Maybe it's a ghost coming to haunt me, or a monster coming to devour my flesh. But it's neither. A white light, ever glowing, pulsates like a heartbeat. I can't stop myself. My blood races. I need to know. *I have to know.*

"Lord Wolfgang," Kronklich calls from behind me, but it is too late. "Wait," he says again but his voice is fading fast as I limp farther away, out of the darkness and into the light. Maybe some miracle will happen to me. Maybe I will be granted mercy one last time. This has happened before and if my inclination is right, I will get to see her again.

"Diana." I call her name, but there is nothing, only the lingering echo of my weak voice. All around me, the eerie glow of peony flowers illuminates the darkness, a trail of them, dozens of them. I keep limping. Kronklich is still calling behind me, but I ignore him. She is here and I am so close.

I come to stop before a massive pile of rocks, where an avalanche fell into the depths of the surrounding dark. There are dozens of stones, but the source of white light glows from underneath the rocks. I begin clearing stone after stone. The boulder I need to get to is trapped under so many. My Diana. She's here. She's here!

Kronklich appears next to me breathing heavily, yet saying nothing. He begins clearing the stones. No words are exchanged.

One after another, we move the stones until there is one left, but it is too heavy for me to move on my own. Kronklich joins my struggle to push the large boulder aside, and as it's wedged from its foundation, it rolls to the bottom of the pile with a dull crunch. The light dims after uncovering the hole and I am left staring down into it, speechless. Kronklich's expression looks confused and he turns to me with a puzzled look. Of course he would. He has never seen it. No one has, except two people.

The Hand of God.

It lies in the dirt, unattended and forgotten. A powerful relic made so simple. Two metal bars bound together by sharp barbed wire.

Picking it up, I hold it before me with one hand. God has a plan for vampires just as he has for humans, to give them a chance at redemption. Was God so merciful? Every ounce of me wants to cast it aside. Such a waste of time. This thing has only caused woe for me.

Turning it over, I feel it is cold and heavy. My finger runs over the dark metal. It is said the ancient relic has the power to vanquish the vampire, to abolish the curse and restore humanity. I have seen it. Egleaseon was proof of that.

A strange sensation washes over me. Something I have not felt in days. Hope. Purpose. It isn't God's presence I feel. Of course it's not. He has abandoned me along with the rest of the world. It seems Bronin was right about one thing.

I look down at the holy relic in my hand and cannot forget how I found it in the first place. "Thank you, Diana."

Kronklich's voice startles me. His hand is like ice on my arm. "Who are you talking to?"

"No one," I say, tucking the device into my belt.

He glances at it and then back at me. "I could really use a cup of tea."

Of course he could. What would I do without Kronklich?

Kronklich's eyes seem to radiate in the dim light of the cavern. "I suppose we should search for a way out, then."

"Indeed," I say, standing up. I know now nothing will stop me from saving my son. Nothing. Not even death. I would trade my soul for his life if I had to.

Rock after rock, we search through the wreckage of the subterranean ruins, hoping to feel a breeze through a crevice or a sign of moss growing on the ground. We search for what seems an eternity until finally our perseverance pays off. There, at the top of a large rock formation, rays of daylight part the darkness.

It has never felt better to see the sun.

END OF BOOK ONE

Egleaseon Ruins

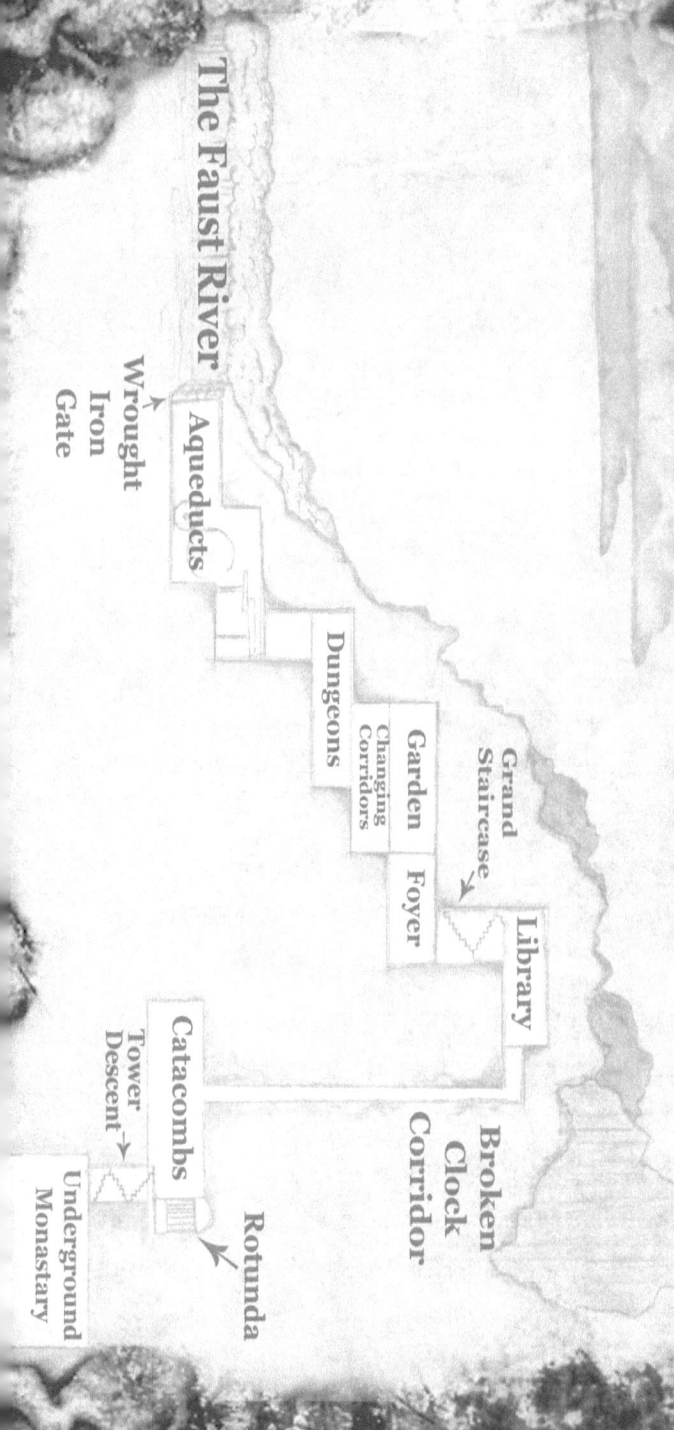

The Faust River

Wrought
Iron
Gate

Aqueducts

Dungeons

Changing
Corridors

Garden

Foyer

Grand
Staircase

Library

Broken
Clock
Corridor

Catacombs

Tower
Descent

Rotunda

Underground
Monastary

ACKNOWLEDGEMENTS

I WOULD LIKE TO TAKE a moment to reminisce on those who have inspired and helped me in the arduous task of creating Wolfgang:

First and foremost, to my wonderful and beautiful D (Diana) who has conveyed her love and ideas about the world of darkness to me. Without your dedication, intuition, and faith, my ambition of completing the book would never have become a reality.

To my lovely London, for reminding me everyday (whether you know it or not) to live life in the fullest and that other worlds do exist.

To Dr. Faustus, for being majestic.

To the following individuals for taking the time to read my work and give your sincere critiques: Marcos Figueroa, Rob & Joni Stewart, (Vampire) Mike Haluska, Mikey Jr. Ralabate.

To my parents, family, and friends, for your loving support and conversations we've had. You know who you are...

I would like to give a special thanks to:

Deborah DeNicola, for taking an expressed interest in my work and offering your editing services. Your insight proved to be an enlightening journey.

Johnathan Gegerson and Nick Reyes, for providing ancient wisdom in promotion and marketing.

George and Kady Young, Mr. and Mrs. Young Senior, Christine Andreason, David Adrian Giralt for your support.

Monica Harman, Julia Johnson-Viola, and Barbara Scanlon, from Bookfuel. Thanks for all your assistance.

Janis Humpage for going above and beyond with your opinions and ideas and your undying dedication in moral support from day one.

A special extra thanks to Bill Fears for helping out in every way possible and having the willingness and patience to work with me on all the artwork inserts, revising the concepts and rendering them to fit the theme. (You understand the true nature of the skull my friend.)

Cheers to all and to those I have yet to meet! 'Till next time....

~ F. D. Gross

Blood of the Father.

The words stick to me like glue. Turning over in my thoughts, again and again. What did it mean?

Crunching through layers of snow, it hurts to breathe the cold mountainous air. Any normal man would stop thinking all together in this situation, trying to survive, but my thoughts never veer from the words Bronin spoke.

Blood of the Father.

Kronklich is not far ahead of me, poking at the snow with his cane, scouting, navigating, ensuring our safety. I look into the blazing white of blizzard off the side of the mountain. My son is not safe. He is somewhere out there. Taken by the evil I loathe and hunted all my life. Seems the tables have turned. I, the hunter, is now hunted. Why my son? Why my blood? The questions spin on and on.

I will not stop until I find answers…

Look for

WOLFGANG: INQUISITION

Book Two of the Wolfgang Chronicles

The hunt for answers continues 2017

F. D. GROSS IS THE author of Wolfgang and the creator of the Wolfgang novel series. Frank lives in South Florida with his girl-friend and daughter and has a cat named after the famous play, Dr. Faustus. When he is not writing, he can be found reading works of classical literature and fantasy, playing music and riding his bike through the woods.

www.Wolfgangchronicles.com
www.facebook.com/Wolfgang.Chronicles
www.twitter.com/GrellDragon

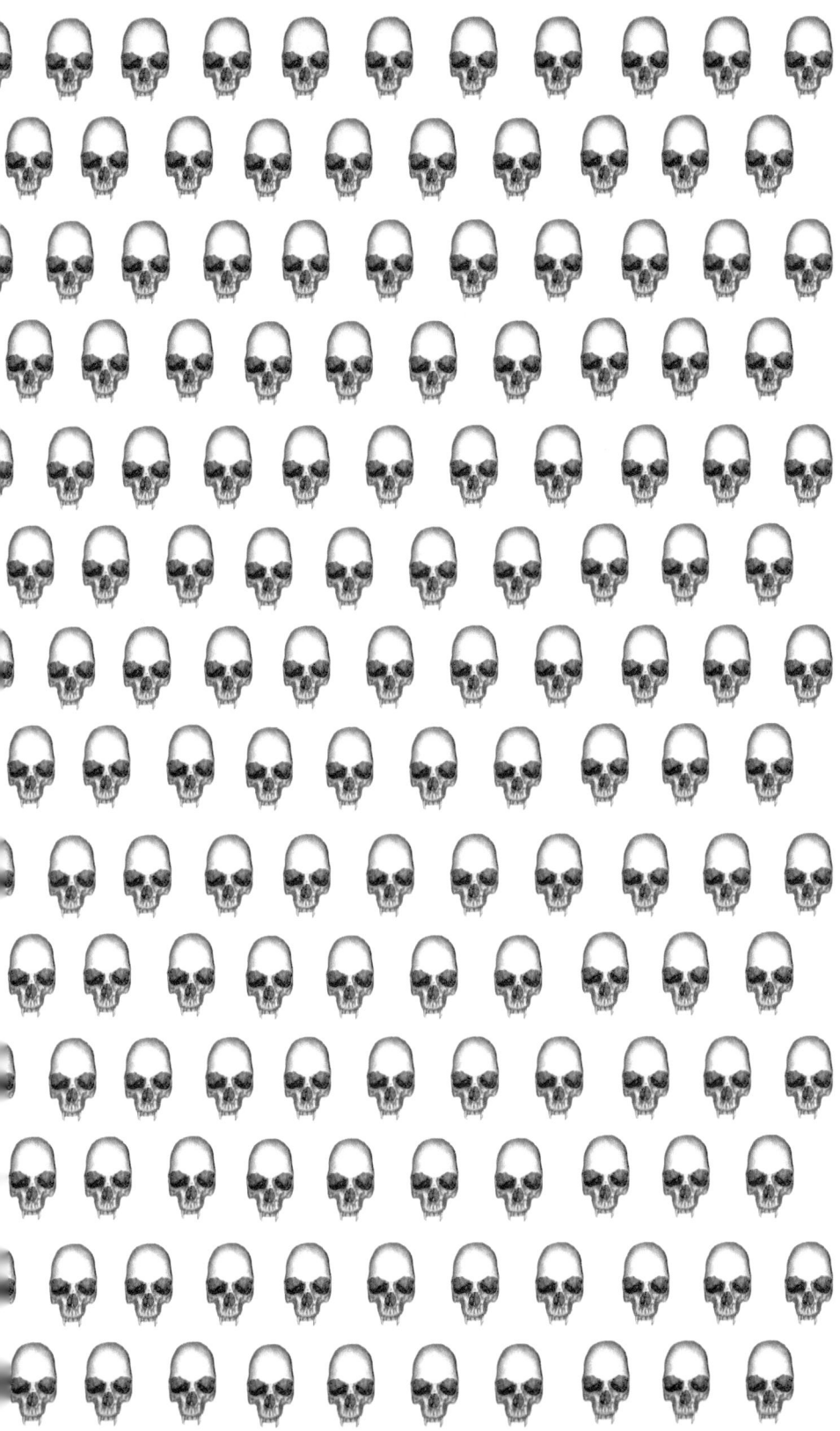

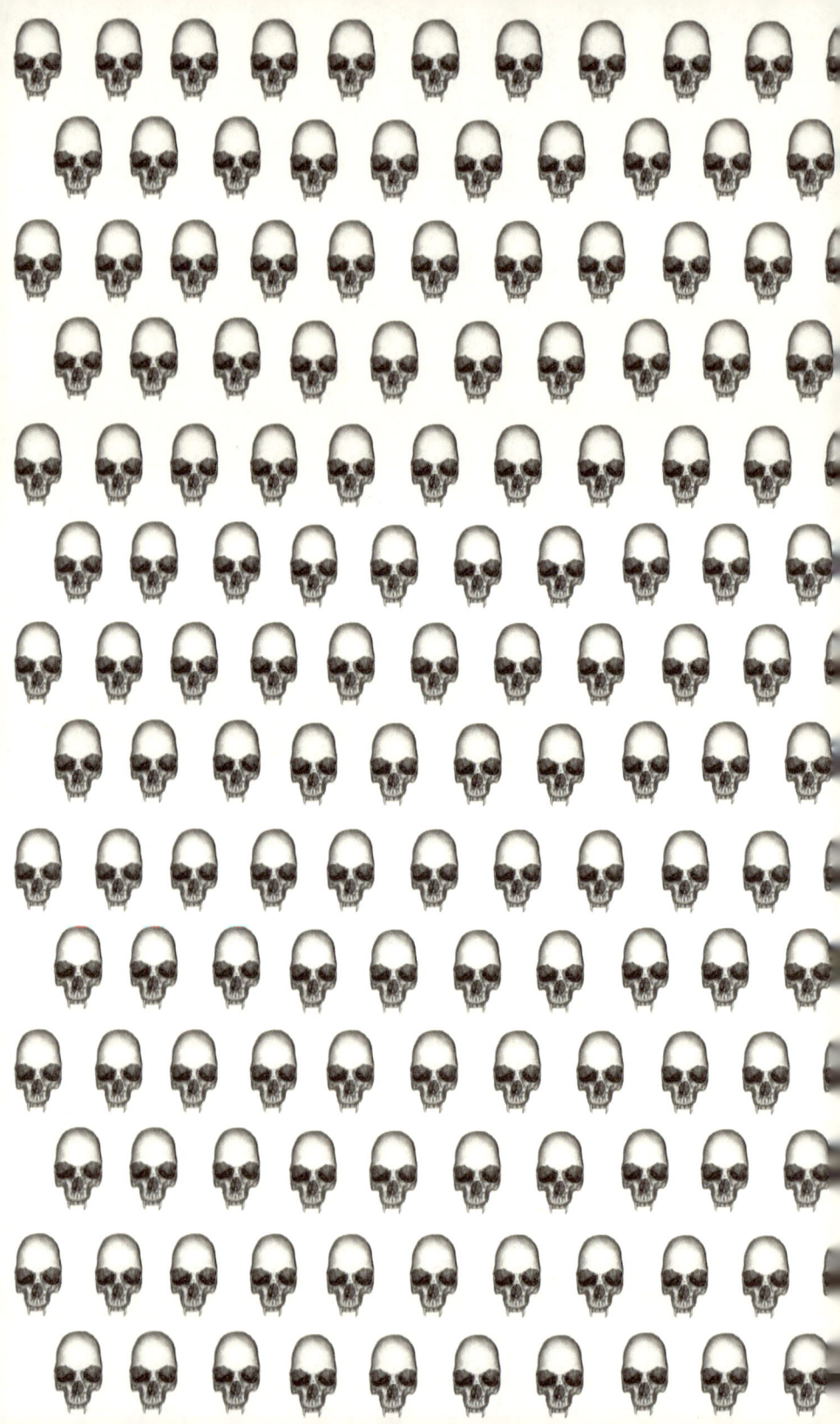